The Ace of
Diamonds Gang

Also by Owen Marshall

The Ace of Diamonds Gang

BY

OWEN MARSHALL

MCINDOE • PUBLISHERS

Published with the assistance of
the Literature Programme of
the QE II Arts Council of New Zealand

ISBN 0 86868 152 0

First published 1993 by
McIndoe • Publishers and printed by John McIndoe Ltd.,
51 Crawford Street, Dunedin, New Zealand.

CONTENTS

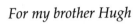

For my brother Hugh

THE MASTER OF BIG JINGLES

I know what it's called now, it's called fennel. Knowing the name doesn't make it what it was however. I see it rarely now. It peers occasionally from the neglected and passing sections, like the face of a small man over the shoulders of others in a crowd. Its fronds are the pale green of hollow glass, and it has a look of pinched resignation, as if it can foresee the evolutionary course before it.

When Creamy Myers and I were young, it was in its prime. There were forests of it pressing in on the town, and it reared up confidently in waxy profusion. The rough strip below the bridge was its heartland, and there Creamy and I had our hut. We could reach it by tunnel tracks from the river bank, and the fence. We built it in the summer which ended our standard four year, and in the summer after that we renewed it in our friendship. The year we finished primary school we restored it again. We cut out the tunnel tracks as usual; so narrow that the top foliage showed no tell-tale gap, and even Rainbow Johnston wouldn't find them. We evicted the hedgehog and its loosely balled nest from the hut, and spread new sacks to mark our occupation. In a biscuit tin we kept the important things, wax-heads, shanghais, tobacco, fishing lines and the tin of cows' teat ointment I found on the bridge.

Fennel is the great home of snails: it is their paradise, nirvana and happy hunting ground. The matchless abundance of the snails was a fascination to us, and a symbol of the place itself. The snails were the scarabs of our own hieroglyphic society, and the snail hunt was the most satisfying of our rituals. From the length, breadth and depth of the river terrace we took them. From time to time one of us would return, and lift his shirt from his trousers, to tumble the catch into the biscuit tin. When we had a massed heap of them, perhaps 150 or more, we would sit in the hut and anoint them. We used the cows' teat vaseline; rubbing it on the shells to darken the pattern and make them shine. We would lie the snails in handfuls amongst the fennel, just off the sacks, in the penumbral green light. As we watched the snails would begin their ceremonial dispersal: large and small, sly and bold, all with the patterns of their shells waxed and gleaming. Scores of snails, each with its own set angle of direction. The gradual, myriad intersection of the planes of their escape through the fennel was like an abacus of three dimensions.

The friendship of Creamy and myself was the smallest and strongest of several circles. We often played with Arty and Lloyd, and there were other faces that we expected at other times. If we went swimming at the town baths for instance, we joined up with the Rosenberg twins. They didn't seem to do much else but swim. But sometimes when Creamy and I were sick of what the others were doing, or after school when we'd rather be alone, then we'd make our signal, just a movement of the head, that meant we'd meet later at the hut. The hut was something apart from the rest of the world. In its life were only Creamy and me. As long as we agreed, our word was law, and no conventions but our own were followed.

I remember just when Creamy told me about going to Technical. We'd had a snail hunt, and were sitting by the river to wash. Creamy had his shirt off, and the snail tracks glistened on his chest. The linear droppings, inoffensively small, clung there too. 'Dad told me I'm not going to Boys' High after all,' he said. 'He's sending me to Tech.' Creamy voice was doubtful, as if he wasn't sure if it marked an important decision or not.

'But I thought we were all going to High?'

Creamy leant into the shingle of the river. He supported himself on his arms, and lifted first one hand then the other to wash his chest. 'Dad said if I'm going into the garage with him, I need the Tech courses. He doesn't go much on languages and stuff.' Creamy had a broad, almost oriental face, and his upper lip was unusually full. It sat slightly over the bottom lip, and gave his face an expression of thoughtful drollery.

'I suppose after school we'll be able to do things together just the same. Maybe it's just like being in different classes at the same school.' I had a premonition though that Creamy's father had done something which would harm us.

'I did try to get Dad to change his mind,' said Creamy. He said it almost as if he wanted it recorded; lest some time in the future he might be blamed for not putting up more of a fight. Creamy flexed his arms, and recoiled with easy grace out of the water. He pulled the back of his trousers down, and showed the marks of a hiding. 'I did try,' said Creamy, and his upper lip quirked a little at the understatement.

'I don't see why it should make that much difference.' I could say that because it was weeks away in any case. When you are thirteen, nothing that is weeks away can be taken seriously. Creamy and I controlled time in those days; we could spin out one summer's day for an eternity of experience.

'Maybe I'll play against you in football,' said Creamy speculatively.

'I'll cut you down if you do.' We smiled, and Creamy skipped the stones across the surface of the river with a flick of his wrist. The sun dried the water from us, and snapped the broom pods like an ambush on the other side of the river. Already I was surprised at my innocence in thinking that all my friends must go like myself to the High School.

Time made no headway against us that summer; not while we were together. But then my family went on holiday to the Queen Charlotte Sounds, and I returned to find the world moved on. The new term was before us, and Creamy was indeed going to the Tech, and I to the High.

I didn't see Creamy after school during the first week, and on Saturday when we went after lizards on the slopes behind the reservoir, we didn't wear uniform. But the next Tuesday we met at the hut, and the nature of our division was apparent. Although I should have expected it, Creamy's Tech uniform was a blow. His grey trousers to my navy blue; his banded socks and cap, distinct in a separate allegiance. Creamy was never deceived by outward appearance. A smile spread out under his full upper lip, and creased his tanned face. 'I see you've lost your knob, too,' he said, and lightly touched the top of his cap.

'The fourth formers tore them off. Initiation,' I said.

'Same with us.' It was typical of Creamy that he should notice first about our uniforms a subtlety we had in common; whereas I couldn't help seeing us from the outside. Even my friendship with Creamy hadn't given me a totally personal view. Creamy didn't mention the uniforms again. We left our caps with our shoes and socks in the hut, and waded in the river to catch crayfish. As long as we maintained the old life separate from the new, then both could exist. It was like those studies I did at High School, about the primitive societies existing for hundreds of years, and then collapsing when the white man came. Creamy and I couldn't change much in the old way, because our ideas came from different sources that year. Sooner or later the white man would come to all the pagan societies of our youth.

I never sat down to think it out, but if I had, it must have seemed that as Creamy and I had held our friendship through the end of that summer, and the first term at our new schools, then there was no reason why we shouldn't go on. That wasn't the way of it however. In the winter months I didn't see much of Creamy. The days were short, and the rugby practices we went to almost always came on different nights. I made new friends too; like big Mathew and Ken Marsden. When I was with Creamy, I sometimes found myself assuming that he knew all about High, and then half-way through some story I'd realize that it must have been meaningless to him. Creamy never showed any impatience. Creamy had a natural and attractive courtesy. He would sit there smiling, his expanding lip faintly frog-like, and say, 'He sounds a real hard case,' or, 'I wish I'd seen that.' Unless I asked him, he never said much about Tech. The odd thing perhaps about sport, or the time he saw Rainbow Johnston smash the windows in the gym. Rainbow was the baron of all our childhood fiefdoms. He had a job at the pie-cart in the evenings, and made more money by stealing milk coupons. Birds stopped singing when Rainbow came past. He knew how to twist an arm till the tears came, did Rainbow, and it was said he made little kids put their hands in his trousers.

In the third term, when it became summer again, we began going back to the river. Not just Creamy and me any more though, for I'd grown accustomed to spending my time with Mathew and Ken. The first time I took them to the hut, Arty was with us too. Arty knew Creamy from primary school, but Mathew and Ken didn't. I could see them measuring themselves against Creamy, as the afternoon went on. Creamy didn't seem to mind; Creamy liked a challenge in his own unassuming way. Creamy could stand measurement beside anyone I knew.

The mentality of youth is able to unhook its jaws like a snake, and swallow up whole antelopes of experience. Youth is a time for excess; for breaking through the ice to swim, for heaping up a mountain of anointed snails from the fennel, for sledging until your hands are bleeding from the ropes, and sunstroke smites you down. Youth is a time for crazes; hula-hoops and under-water goggles, bubble gum and three-D cardboard viewers.

But that year it was knuckle bones. The year when Creamy and my new High School friends met, it was knuckle bones. Knuckle bones had risen obscurely, like an Asian plague, and swept as an epidemic through our world — brief and spectacular. Creamy excelled at knuckle bones of course: Creamy was insolently good at knuckle bones. Like chickens about a hen, the knuckle bones grouped and disbanded, came and went round Creamy's hand. Creamy had begun with plastic knuckle bones. The soft drink colours of the pieces would rise and fall, collect and separate, at Creamy's behest. He won an aluminium set in the Bible class competition. The aluminium ones were heavier and didn't ricochet. Creamy was even better with the aluminium ones. Cutting cabbages, camels, swatting flies, clicks, little jingles, through the arch, goliath, horses in the stable; Creamy mastered them all.

Creamy's expression didn't change when Ken challenged him to knuckle bones. He seemed interested in my new friends. His fair hair hung over his forehead, and his complex face was squinting in the sun. Ken was good at knuckle bones; as good as me, but he wouldn't beat Creamy I knew. Creamy was a golden boy, and it's useless to envy those the gods have blessed. Ken and he went right through knuckles bones twice without any faults. 'What do you think is the hardest of all?' said Creamy. Ken considered. He pushed the knuckle bones about the ground with his finger as he thought.

'I reckon the big jingles,' he said.

'Ten big jingles on the go,' said Creamy. 'I challenge you to ten big jingles without a fault.'

'You go first then,' said Arty. 'You go first and if you make a mistake then Ken wins.'

'All right,' said Creamy. The injustice of it didn't seem to worry him. He started out as smoothly as ever, allowing no time for tension to gather. His rhythm didn't vary, and his broad face was relaxed.

'That's good going,' said Mathew when Creamy had finished, and Ken had failed to match him.

'They're small though, these aluminium ones.' Arty seemed jealous of the praise. 'Smaller than the real or plastic knuckle bones. It's a big advantage to have them small in big jingles.'

'Stiff,' said Creamy.

Later in the afternoon we found ourselves fooling about by the bridge. Along the underside of the bridge was a pipe which Creamy and I sometimes crossed to prove we could do it. 'Creamy and I often climb across that,' I told the others. They looked at it in silence.

'Shall we do it now?' said Mathew at last. He thought he was strong enough to try anything.

There's no dichotomy of body and spirit when you're young. Adults see the body as an enemy, or a vehicle to be apprehensively maintained. There's just you, when you're young; flesh and spirit are indivisible. For Creamy and I then, for all of us in youth, any failure in body was a failure of the spirit too. Creamy went first. As always when he was concentrating, his lunar upper lip seemed more obvious, the humorous expression of his face more pronounced, as though he were awaiting the punch line of some unfolding joke. He leant out, and took hold of the pipe. He moved his grip about, as a gymnast does to let his hands know the nature of the task, then he swung under the pipe, and began hand over hand to work his way to the central bridge support. He used his legs as a pendulum, so that the weight of his body was transferred easily from one hand to the other as he moved. When he reached the centre support, Creamy rested in the crook of its timbers, and looked down to the river. Then he carried on, hanging and swaying below the pipe, becoming smaller in silhouette against the far bank as he went.

'Seems easy enough,' said Arty.

'You go next then,' said Ken. Arty measured the drop between Creamy's swaying figure and the river beneath.

'I would,' he said. 'I would, but I've got this chest congestion. I see the doctor about it.'

'Sure.'

Mathew could only think about one thing at a time, and as he was busy watching Creamy he found himself next in line for the pipe. The rest of us by slight manoeuvrings had got behind him. 'It's me then,' said Mathew. He took a grip and his body flopped down beneath the pipe, and stopped with a jerk. His up-stretched arms were pulled well clear of his jersey, and his hands were clamped onto the pipe. The crossing was an exercise in sheer strength for Mathew; he pulled himself along clumsily, and his legs hung down like fence posts below this thick body. I went next. I didn't want Arty in front of me in case he froze, and I couldn't get past. The few feet just before the central support were the worst, for if I looked down there I could see the concrete base of the timber supports on which I'd fall, instead of into the water. I used to count the number of swings I made just there; one, two, three, four, until I was able to put my feet on the wooden supports. The second half wasn't so bad because at the end if you were tired, you could drop off onto the grassy bank which rose up towards the underside of the bridge.

Arty and Ken didn't go over at all. Arty pretended he'd seen a big trout in the hole beneath the bridge, and he and Ken went down and poked under the bank with a stick. When we came back over the bridge, we couldn't see any big trout in the hole. 'Want to go over the pipe again?' said Creamy mildly.

'That's hard work, that.' Mathew was always honest.

'Good though,' said Creamy.

As we scuffed about in the shingle at the end of the bridge, a horse and rider came past. The horse paused, and with flaunting tail deposited vast rolls of waste. Mathew watched the horse with awe. 'I bet horses are the biggest shitters around,' he said.

'No, in proportion guinea pigs are far greater shitters,' said Creamy.

'Guinea pigs?'

'Yeah, in proportion they are.'

'Rabbits are good shitters,' said Arty.

'I don't see how anything could beat horses and elephants,' said Ken. As an ally he weakened Mathew's argument. The rest of us recognised the subtlety of Creamy's reasoning.

'Guineas are by far the best shitters in proportion.' Creamy knew he was right. 'Imagine a guinea pig as big as a horse. Now there would be a shitter.'

'Yeah,' said Mathew in wonder, and capitulation.

We had a swim, and threw fennel spears at each other during the rest of the afternoon. We forgot about the time, and Ken's sister came looking for him. She left her bike by the road, and came down to the fence, calling out for Ken. 'You've got to come home,' she said. Her breasts caused furrows across the material of her blouse.

'Have you been eating too much or something,' said Arty. We had a good laugh at that witticism. 'Turning into a moo-vie star,' continued Arty, pleased with his reception. He tucked his thumbs into his shirt, and paraded before her and us.

'Oh, get lost,' she said. She began to go back up the bank towards the road. 'You'd better come, Ken. You know what'll happen,' she said.

'Hubba hubba, ding ding, look at the tits on that thing,' we sang.

'Watch out for Rainbow Johnston,' I called out.

'Hey, Rainbow, here she is.'

'Quick Rainbow.'

For the first time Ken's sister seemed flustered. She looked back along the river bank, and then hurried on to her bike. I don't know why I called out about Rainbow. Perhaps in looking at her smooth legs and breasts, I found some part of Rainbow in myself; some desire to reach out and pinch her, or twist her arm, or worse.

Ken stayed a little longer, trying to show he wasn't afraid of being late, but we soon all began straggling back down the road. Creamy and I walked the last part together. 'I'm looking forward to the full summer,' I said. Creamy agreed. He played with his knuckle bones, and whistled as he walked, his upper lip funnelling out and creating a very clear, penetrating whistle. His shoes, worn by water and grass during the afternoon, were almost white at the toes. Creamy stopped whistling, and asked me if Ken and Mathew were the two I liked best at High School. I told him I quite liked them.

'I'm getting sick of Arty,' said Creamy thoughtfully. 'You know that. I'm finding Arty pretty much of a pill.'

'So am I,' I said. Creamy tossed his aluminium knuckle bones up and down again in the palm of his hand. We were nearly at the street where Creamy turned off. 'You didn't mind Ken and Mathew being there?' I asked him. Creamy didn't give any glib answer. He walked on for a while.

'I suppose it's selfish to just have one or two friends,' he said. 'I suppose as you get older, you meet more and more people and make friends with them. Only I don't seem to find as many as you. There's an awful lot like Arty.'

As Creamy went off home, I thought about that; for the first time I realized that despite being good at everything, Creamy didn't have that many friends. Being good at everything was in itself a disadvantage even. That's what was the matter with Arty; he resented Creamy's ability. Somewhere, he'd like to see Creamy take a fall.

The next Saturday I went again. Ken couldn't come, but Mathew and Arty did. I hadn't seen Creamy, but I thought he'd be there. He had another Tech boy with him. None of us knew him. He had eyebrows that grew right across the top of his nose. I'd never seen anyone with one long eyebrow like that before. His name was Warwick Masters. When he thought something was funny, he let his head fall forward, bouncing on his chest, and gave a snuffling laugh on the indrawn breath.

Creamy and I hadn't had any snail hunts that summer. No decision was made not to, we just didn't do it. As third formers we were growing out of snail hunts, and on to more fitting things like knuckle bones, and calling hubba hubba, ding ding, at Ken's sister. Yet the way Warwick treated the snails made me so angry I could feel my throat becoming tight. 'Christ almighty,' said Warwick, 'look at these snails.' He reached into the fennel walls of the hut, and plucked out the snails. 'Just look at these snails will you.' He let his head bounce on his chest, and gave his idiotic, sucking laugh. He arranged a line of them by the wall, then smashed each one with his fist. The shells cracked like biscuits, and what was left of the snails seemed to swell up in visceral agony after Warwick's fist was lifted. Creamy made no attempt to stop him; he hardly seemed to notice what he was doing.

'Don't do that,' I said to Warwick.

'Bloody snails.'

'It only makes a mess in the hut.'

'Stiff,' said Warwick. 'That's really stiff.'

'Just leave them alone.'

'Yeah?'

'Yeah.'

'Yeah?'

'Yeah.' The verbal sparring quickened into a semblance of humour, and Warwick bounced his head and laughed.

'Anyway,' said Arty, 'I don't think you Tech guys should come to the hut.'

'It's always been my hut too,' said Creamy seriously. Three summers are an accepted eternity when one is young.

'It's got to be either Tech or High ground,' said Mathew. He liked things simple for his own peace of mind. 'All the places got to be either Tech or High.' Mathew's simplicity had found the truth. All the places that mattered in our town were either High or Tech ground. The territories were marked, and only the adults in their naivety were unaware. My father never understood why I wouldn't take the short cut through the timber yard on my way to school.

'This side of the bridge is ours,' said Arty.

'But it's closest to the Tech swimming hole.'

'Stiff.'

Warwick picked up some of the squashed snails and quickly wiped them down Arty's face, then crashed away through the fennel a few paces, and stood bouncing his head and snorting. Creamy's subtle and unique face creased with delight, but he made no movement. Arty flung the remaining mess of snails at him, and urged Mathew to grab him. 'Grab him Mathew, grab him.' Creamy dodged Mathew's first clumsy attempt; he seemed as if he were about to say something, but Arty got in first. 'High onto Tech,' he shouted.

'Yeah,' I heard myself say, but without reason. It seemed to come from a surface part of me, and not deeper where I thought things out. Creamy slipped from the hut, and stood with Warwick.

'For today you mean,' he said smiling. Creamy loved a battle.

'For always,' said Arty. Arty was pleased that at last he had something over Creamy. Creamy was Tech, and the rest of us were High. Creamy was quicker, stronger, better at knuckle bones and swinging under the bridge, a true friend, but he was Tech. Arty, like most weak people, enjoyed advantages he couldn't himself create. 'For always. No more Tech farts on the bank. Fight you for it.'

It was three onto two, but that didn't worry Creamy. He had a sense of occasion though, did Creamy. If it had to be Tech against High after all, then it should be done on a fitting scale. 'Thursday night then,' said Creamy. His full upper lip expanded as he thought about it, and his eyes took on the visionary look with which he regarded his schemes. A look that hinted at the appreciation of more colours than existed in the spectrums of the rest of us. 'On Thursday after school we'll have the full fight between Tech and High for the bank. You get all you can, and we'll meet you. All out war.'

'I don't know,' said Arty. 'Maybe we should set rules and numbers.' Arty's brief moment of initiative was over; Creamy had as always taken control.

'All out war,' he repeated, and Warwick's head bounced and his laugh sounded through the fennel.

'Is it really all out war?' I said. I could see Creamy's face not many paces away, but he didn't answer. 'All out?' I said. Creamy's face was relaxed and droll; so difficult to read.

'Full scale,' cried Warwick. 'Tech against High.' And still Creamy didn't answer.

'We'll win easily,' said Mathew. 'We can round up a dozen or more easily.'

'Look out for Rainbow Johnston, that's all,' called Warwick. He went off laughing, to follow Creamy, who had turned away and begun walking towards the fence below the bridge.

I watched Creamy climb up the road with Warwick, and I knew it had happened. I knew that him going to Tech and me going to High had ruined our friendship after all. I looked at Arty and Mathew standing by the hut, and I knew that neither of them was half the friend that Creamy had been. 'Do you think they'll really get Rainbow?' said Arty hollowly.

'I've heard things about Rainbow. I think we need plenty of guys.' Mathew's slow logic was depressing.

'Can we get enough though?' said Arty.

'Jesus, Arty,' I said, 'will you stop moaning.'

That week at school we started getting as many allies as we could. Arty wrote the names down on the back of his pad. He had two lists — one headed possibles and one headed probables, like trial teams. There were some names in the possibles that I hardly knew. Not even all the probables were at the gate after school on Thursday though. Arty himself didn't show up until we were just about to go. We told him he was trying to get out of it. 'No I'm not. I'm coming; of course I'm coming. I just had to put off other things, that's all. What do you think of this stick!' Arty had a short piece of sawn timber. He hit it against the fives courts, and then tried not to show that he'd jarred his hand. 'I reckon I'm ready,' he said.

We began walking towards the river, but a car drew up over the road, and the man driving it called out to Arty. It was Arty's father. Arty went over and talked with him, then came partly back. 'Wouldn't you know it,' he said. 'I've got to go up to the hospital for my tests. It has to be tonight.' With Arty's father watching from the car, it wasn't any use saying much. 'Maybe the Tech will be there again tomorrow night. I'll be right for tomorrow.'

'Sure,' said Ken. Arty walked over the road quickly. As he got into the car he let his stick slip onto the roadway.

'He rang his dad,' said Lloyd. 'That's what he did.' Arty couldn't meet our eyes as the car pulled away.

'What a dunny brush he turned out to be,' said Mathew, and we laughed. I was on the point of telling them what Creamy had said about Arty, Creamy had him picked all right, then I remembered that Creamy had become the enemy.

That left seven of us. Mathew, Ken, Lloyd, Buzz Swanson and the Rosenbergs. And me of course. As we got closer to the bridge I had a strange feeling that our group was becoming smaller, although the number remained the same. Ken was walking beside me, and I saw how frail he was. His legs were so thin they seemed swollen at the knees to accommodate the joints. He had little, white teeth that looked as if they were his first set. Even as Ken smiled at me, I thought to myself that he was going to be useless. I didn't want to be by Ken when we were fighting. I'd keep by Mathew. Mathew's dirty knees were comfortingly large, and he plodded on resolutely. 'Perhaps we should scout around first, and find out how many of them there are,' I said to Mathew.

'I've got to be home by half-past five,' said Ken. I bet you do Ken, I bet you do, I thought. I resolved that not only would I stick with Mathew when it started, I'd make sure Ken wasn't protecting my back. I had some idea it was going to be like the musketeers of Dumas; us back to back against the odds of the Tech boys.

We stood on the raised road leading up to the bridge, and looked over the bank from the fence, across the frothing fennel to the greywacke shingle of the river bed, where the larger stones crouched like rabbits in the afternoon sun. Creamy stepped out from the cover of the willows two hundred yards away. He raised one arm slowly, and lowered it again. It caught the significance of our presence, as a hawk becomes the sky. It had nothing to do with friendship or compromise: it was a sign of recognition. It was a sign of deeper cognizance too, in that we were there. Unlike Arty and the others on the list, we had come. So Creamy acknowledged our equality of hostility.

Life was drama when we were young. The power of it made Lloyd's voice shake when he reminded us to keep together as we broke our way through the fennel. Creamy watched us coming for a bit, then disappeared behind the willows. 'Where are they?' said Ken. They were below the bank, where the terrace met the river bed. As if to answer Ken's question, they began throwing stones which snicked through the fennel.

'Let's head for the willows,' I said. The Tech harried us as we went. I could hear Warwick's indrawn laugh, and I had a desultory stick fight with a boy who used to be in cubs with me. The Rosenberg twins were the best fighters on our side. They probably had the least notion as to why we were there in the first place, but they were the best fighters all right. They seemed to fight intuitively as one person; four arms and four feet. They rolled one Tech kid over the bank, and winded him on the shingle below. Mathew seemed unable to catch anyone to fight in this sort of guerrilla warfare. Nobody took him on, but he was too slow to take on anybody himself. He kept moving towards the willows, and we skirmished about him.

I think the whole thing might have petered out, if Rainbow hadn't come. Even in an all out fight there were rules: you knew that no-one would deliberately poke anything in your eye, or hold your head under water longer than you could hold your breath. Rainbow was different. He liked to hurt people did Rainbow. He stepped up on to the bank by the willows, and halted our forward progress. He had a thick stick. 'So it's Tech against High,' said Rainbow. His features were gathered closely on his round head, like sprout marks on a coconut. He held the stick in front of Ken, and Ken stopped. The rest of us did nothing. We did nothing not just because Rainbow Johnston was a fifth former, but because he was Rainbow Johnston. And deep down we were glad he'd picked on Ken , and not on us.

'I'm pax,' said Ken. It was the best he could think of, and its incongruity set the Tech guys laughing.

'Pax!' said Rainbow bitterly. 'We don't have any pax between Tech and High.' He drew back his stick, and speared it out at Ken, catching him on the side of the chest. Ken fell on his back, and as his head hit the soft grass his hair flopped away from his face, making him seem even younger.

'Ah, Jesus,' said Ken, and he got up and felt his side where he'd been struck. He laughed shakily, and picked up his own stick in a show of defiance. Then he dropped his stick again, and began to cry. He slumped down on his knees and held his side. He arched his back and squeezed his eyes closed with the pain.

'We've won', said Creamy, before anyone else could think of a reaction to what had happened. Rainbow motioned with his stick towards the rest of us. 'We've won,' repeated Creamy quietly. 'You can stay and play in the hut, Rainbow.' Creamy had found the right note as ever. With the fight declared over, Rainbow felt a bit ashamed to be with third formers. He vaulted over the sagging willow trunk onto the river bed, and slouched off upstream. 'See you, Rainbow,' said Creamy.

'Yeah,' said Rainbow.

Ken was still crying. There was some blood showing through his shirt from the graze, and Mathew and I helped him up. We began to go back to the bridge through the fennel. 'They can't come here again, Creamy, can they?' called out Warwick. 'It's Tech now.'

'They can't come here again,' said Creamy. His face was the same; relaxed, and with the upper lip creating the impression of incipient humour. He didn't speak with any special triumph.

We broke down the fennel in our retreat, paying no attention to the tunnels Creamy and I had made. I was glad Tech had won. I joined in the talk about the injustice of Rainbow being there, but I was glad they'd won. It gave a more general explanation for the end of our friendship — Creamy's and mine. There couldn't be any personal betrayal when it was a matter of Tech and High; a commitment to a cause. Ken was still crying, but with greater artifice as his sense of heroism grew. He leant to one side, and he held his shirt out so it wouldn't stick to his graze. The fennel fronds were like miniature conifers, smaller and smaller, each in the join of the other as marsupial embryos in a pouch. The oddly coastal smell of the crushed fennel was all about us. 'I don't know that we lost, not really fair and square,' said Mathew. 'If Rainbow hadn't been there I mean.' They could say what they liked, but for myself I knew I'd lost all right. And it was worse that as I climbed from the fennel, up on to the road, I could understand what it was I'd lost and why.

THE FAT BOY

The men coming from the railway yards were the first to notice the fat boy. He stood beneath the overhead bridge, amongst the cars illegally parked there. He had both hands in the pockets of his short pants and the strain of that plus his heavy thighs made the flap of his fly gape. The fat boy watched the passers-by with the froglike, faintly enquiring look that the faces of fat boys have. The fat boy's hair was amazingly fair and straight; it shone with nourishment; it was straight and oddly medieval.

The men were leaving at twenty past four. It was a conventional extension of the time for washing up that their union had obtained. They resented the fat boy's regard day after day. They were sure that he was stealing from the cars, and it was just as well they were coming past early to watch him, they said. Sometimes they would shout at the fat boy and tell him to get lost, as they walked in their overalls along the black margin of the track past the old gasworks. Seventeen thousand dollars worth of railway property was found missing when the audit was made. The men knew it was outsiders. They remembered the fat boy. The fat kid is the look-out for the ring taking all the stuff, they told the management. Dozens of workers could swear to having seen the fat boy. They went looking for him but he wasn't to be found beneath the overhead bridge any more.

Instead the fat boy began to frequent McNulty's warehouse in Cully Street. Even through the cracked and stained windows the staff could see him standing by the side of the building where the bicycles were left. Sometimes he would kick at the clumps of weeds which grew in the broken pavement there; sometimes he would puff his fat cheeks and blow out little explosions of air; sometimes he would just stand with his hands in his pockets and look at the warehouse as if to impress it on his mind. He had a habit of pulling his mouth to one side, as if biting the skin on the inside of his cheek the way children do. Often in school time he was there. Sometimes even in the rain he was there. The rain glistened on his round cheeks and seemed to shrink his pants so that the lining turned up at the leg holes. The new girl looked out and said he looked as if he was crying. The owner said he'd make him cry all right. He was sick of ordering him away, the owner said.

McNulty's warehouse burnt down in November. The owner made particular mention to the police of the fat boy, but when McNulty's built again in a better area with the insurance money the fat boy never appeared. The paper reported what the owner said about the fat boy. The railway men said it was the same fat boy all right. They said the fat kid was somehow tied up in a lot of the crime going on.

The fat boy seemed to be in uniform, but although he was clearly seen by many people there was no agreement as to his school or family. Some said his socks had the blue diamonds of Marsden High, but others said the blue was in the bands of College. The fat boy had thick legs with no apparent muscles, and they didn't narrow to the ankle. If just his legs could have been turned upside down no-one would ever know it. When the fat boy lifted his brows enquiringly, one crease would form in the smooth, thick skin of his forehead.

The fat boy seemed to be a harbinger of trouble. The fat boy walked behind old Mrs Denzil on her way home from the shopping centre, and he loitered in the shade of her wooden fence, which was draped with dark convolvulus leaves and its pale flowers. The police maintained a quiet watch on the house in case the fat boy came again. On the third night someone broke into Mrs Denzil's house and tied her upside down in the washtub. Her Victorian cameo brooch was stolen, together with the tinned food she hoarded, and eighty-four-year-old Mrs Denzil was left tied upside down in the tub with a tennis ball in her mouth to block her breathing. Oh, that fat boy, they said: even murder, they said. That fat boy was so much more evil than their own sons. There wasn't anything that the fat boy wouldn't do was there, they said.

Nigel Lammerton saw the fat boy on the night he was arrested for beating his wife. Lammerton told the police that when he returned from the hotel he saw the fat boy on the porch of his home, and that his wife couldn't explain why. Lammerton said that he saw the fat boy looking in the window at them while they argued, but that when he ran outside the fat boy was gone. It was the fat boy, and the medication that he had been taking, that made him lose control, Nigel Lammerton told the court. Mrs Lammerton agreed with everything her husband said about the fat boy.

The fat boy could not be found for questioning, but then no-one had ever known the fat boy to say anything. He just watched. The paper said he was malevolent. No-one likes a fat kid staring at them all the time. Lammerton said that everyone was entitled to privacy without a fat kid staring at him. The fat boy had the knack of being where he was least desired.

There was a certain effrontery about the fat boy. He appeared in council chambers during the discussion in committee on a special dispensation from the town planning scheme. The deputy-mayor was declaring that no present councillors had any connection with the consortium which had made application. He became aware of the fat boy watching him from the corridor to the Town Clerk's office. The fat boy's fair hair trembled a little as his mouth stretched in a cavernous yawn, and without taking his hands from his pockets he tapped with his shoe at the wainscotting, the way boys do. One of the councillors went from the meeting to confront the fat boy, but he must have slipped away through the offices, the councillor said.

The deputy-mayor thought that in all of his considerable experience he had never seen such a sly one as the fat boy. He said that somehow he could never bring himself to trust a fat boy; just never could bring himself to trust one, he said.

The fat boy was seen at the I.H.C. centre the day before Melanie Lamb was found to be pregnant. The air was warm; sparrows chirped beneath the swaying birch catkins and pecked at a vomited pie in the gutter. The fat boy stood before the railings and held one of the iron bars like a staff. The children smiled at him as he watched, and were content in his presence, but the supervisors saw him there and remembered when the doctor said that Melanie was pregnant. The music teacher who lived next door to the Lambs thought it a very significant recollection. He said that when he came to think of it he recalled the fat boy standing in the evenings by the hedge at the rear of Melanie's house. A very fat, ugly boy, the music teacher said, and everyone agreed that such a unique description fitted the fat boy perfectly and must be him. It was a terrible thing, the music teacher said, to think that the fat boy could take advantage of Melanie's handicap, even if she was physically advanced.

More than any of the other things it was what he did to Melanie Lamb that enabled people to close ranks against the fat boy. They recognized in him a common enemy. Vigilante groups organized from the King Dick and Tasman hotels began searching for the fat boy. Not many days before Christmas they caught up with the fat boy by the gasworks. Artie Compeyson was drowning kittens in the cutting, and saw the fat boy watching, but didn't let on. The fat boy was stolid at the top of the cutting; his pudding face and medieval hair showed clearly in the moonlight and against the grimy storage tanks of the old gasworks. He was still waiting when the vigilantes came, and they surrounded him there in the patches of light and shadow. The fat boy didn't run, or cry out. He watched them converge, his thick legs apart and his hands pushed deep into the pockets of his short trousers. He was sly all right.

They managed to overpower him, they said. Nigel Lammerton with his experience as a wife-beater, got in one or two really good thuds on the fat boy's face before he went down, and the music teacher, who had an educated foot, kicked the fat boy between the legs. Everyone knew the fat boy must be made to pay for what he had done.

No-one seemed to know what happened to the fat boy's body, and such a body wasn't easy to hide. The moon seemed to go behind cloud just as the fat boy fell, and the vigilantes became rather confused after the excitement of the night and the debriefing at the King Dick and the Tasman. Although the police dragged the cutting they found only the sack with kittens in it, and five stolen tyres.

Nearly everyone was relieved that the boy had been got rid of. God, but he was evil, they said, that fat boy; all the things he did. It didn't bear thinking about. And no-one likes a fat boy watching them you know. They shared, amongst other things, a conviction that life would be immeasurably better for them all with the fat boy gone.

THE ACE OF DIAMONDS GANG

As our past recedes we can see only occasional pennons on the high ground, which represent the territory traversed between. So the Ace of Diamonds Gang seems my full boyhood before the uncertainty of adolescence. I recall no peculiar origin; like the heroes of history it arose when it needed to be there.

Always the special moment was when we put on our masks. The triangle of white handkerchief over the lower face, and the red diamond that we'd stamp on with the oil paints that belonged to Bernie's mother. There was *frisson* as each known face became strangely divided. Not handkerchiefs with red diamonds smudged did we acquire, but anonymity, confederacy, a clear exception to approved society. After Boys' Brigade was a favourite time; when lanyards and Christianity had been dispensed with, we would rendezvous in the centre of the old macrocarpa hedge to become the Ace of Diamonds Gang. The night would be moonlit perhaps and we would move off in dispersed formation, keeping in touch by drifting whistles and calls of birds extinct except within the diamond lands. Like wraiths we went said Bernie once. He read a lot did Bernie. Like wraiths, the Ace of Diamonds Gang: if Ashley's farting didn't give us all away.

The Ace of Diamonds Gang was rather like that; subject in practice to mundane deficiencies which threatened the ideal. Ashley's wind, Bernie's glasses and Hec Green having to be in by nine o'clock every night, were the sorts of things. A certain power of imagination was necessary, but for 13-year-olds the source of such power is inexhaustible. We never spent much time in explicit definition of the Gang however — each had his own motivation, his own vision of the Ace of Diamonds Gang, and when we struck in that small town each of us gloried in a quite separate achievement. Dusty Rhodes insisted that the gang be used to intensify his wooing of Anna Nicholson who had the best legs in the school. It was love all right. After watching Anna at the swimming sports, Dusty had a hormone headache so severe that he was away for three days. The Ace of Diamonds Gang picketed Anna Nicholson's front garden sometimes, and when she came back from music practices called from the bushes and tossed acorns up to her window. Dusty considered this a normal form of courtship, and the rest of us had not sufficient experience to suggest alternatives. When Anna's father came out with torch and fury, we would drift wraith-like deeper into the shrubbery, not of course from fear, but to give him a taste of the menacing elusiveness of the Ace of Diamonds Gang when true love was thwarted. Dusty could never understand why Anna Nicholson didn't fall for him. The unbearable passion of first love rarely has any relevance to the response of the other party.

For Bernie and me the Ace of Diamonds Gang was more a life warp to escape from being 13 years old in a provincial town; a chance to conjure heroism, to strike a pose, to create mysteries in which to dwell. We cut the backs off some Christmas cards, and stamped them with the red diamond. We left one at the scene of each of our exploits, just as in the books we read. The senior sergeant would pin them in his incident board we were sure, and his staff would attempt to work out a *modus operandi*.

So it was something of a let down to return to Seddon Park weeks after we had painted challenges there, and find the Ace of Diamonds card still there, weathered on the side of the cricket shed. 'They've given up, that's what,' said Dusty.

'That's it all right. They've given up,' said Ashley.

'Perhaps it's still under surveillance,' said Bernie. It was a good word — surveillance, but even it could not impose conviction in that warm morning with the playing fields dipping to the willows, and a harrier club spread in the distance.

'We haven't actually done much lately,' admitted Ashley, who was sitting downwind a little. 'As a gang I mean.' We lay in the grass, shading our eyes with our hands, and attempting to justify the lack of daring in recent excursions of the Ace of Diamonds Gang.

Dusty suggested we spend time drilling a hole in the girls' changing sheds, but the rest of us wanted a cause of greater daring and less obvious connection with our own interest. 'My father told me Jorgesson poisoned Mrs Elder's Alsatian because it kept him awake at night,' said Ashley. Jorgesson ran the second-hand yard, and his enmity could be relied on. He had cuffed Dusty's head for cheek, and once set the police on us after seeing us on the stacks of the timber yard. And he gave us wretched prices for any lead or copper we scrounged because he had the monopoly as the only scrap dealer in town. Sometimes we retrieved the stuff from his yard and sold it to him twice over to gain a fair price by simple addition, but even retaliatory dishonesty didn't remove our resentment.

'Hey, Jorgesson,' repeated Dusty. To defy Jorgesson was grand enough to be a reaffirmation of the principles of the Ace of Diamonds Gang, and Dusty agreed to hold in abeyance further collective effort to seduce Anna Nicholson, and the spy-hole in the sheds.

'Let's raid the place and leave a calling card,' said Bernie, raising a small, clenched fist. 'Strike and vanish, vengeance accomplished; the Ace of Diamonds Gang.' It was Bernie who usually provided the linguistic motifs for the gang.

'Christ, yes,' said Hec, 'but I'll have to be back by nine remember.'

In the fastness of the macrocarpa we met on Wednesday evening; looked out into the soft, eternal twilight of summer. We linked thumbs to make our pledge and put on our Ace of Diamonds masks. Just a handkerchief and a change of mind. The mantle of secret brotherhood then fell upon us — oh, it was fish Christians in the catacombs, the Black Hand, Jacobites, the Scarlet Pimpernel. It was the League of Spartacus, the Boxers: it was Kipling's bazaar. I felt a small part of history's perpetual alternative as we ran through the Marlborough evening.

Jorgesson's was in that part of the town which was never very busy; off the main street and down toward the warehouses. On one side of his yard was a panelbeater's, on the other a vacant section, then the timber yard. When night came all such lands reverted to the domain of the Ace of Diamonds Gang. We scaled the stepped pyramids of the timber yard, and made inventory of Jorgesson Traders. It resembled a field hospital in a desperate war of machines: the corpses and the parts heaped in rough classification as they came in. The ground was toxic and stained with oils, rust, and the juices of dismembered machines. There were heaps of taps like discarded hands, radiators, bumpers, fan units, old bricks, used

sinks, ceramic fire surrounds, short blocks, coppers, windows, roof-
ing iron, bottle castles in green and brown, heaps of worn tyres like
bitter, dark intestines. Amidst all the obsolescence were a few new
kitset patio chairs assembled by Jorgesson during his quiet times.
Much of the stock was exposed to take its chances beneath the
spartan sky; a second category lay in an open-sided shed and its
progressively diminishing lean-tos. We knew that the most precious
and portable items festooned Jorgesson's army hut, so that it was a
labyrinthine progress for him to make the short journey from his
desk and cashbox to the door.

There seemed a dim light from the hut as we watched from our
battlements. 'He must still be there,' said Hec. Ashley perfumed the
night in response to heightened and unexpected tension.

'But we'll still go,' I said.

'We should reconnoitre in strength,' advised Bernie. His glasses
glinted a moment in the last light of the evening. We steadied
ourselves in the timber, and locked our thumbs again in pledge.

So did we move wraith-like across the rough section between the
timber yard and Jorgesson's, scouts taking post then others fading
forward. We hand-cupped each other over the fence, drew up Hec
as the last, and stood amongst Jorgesson's darkened possessions.
The one window in the army hut showed light like the pale yellow
yolk of a battery egg. It was above head height and we pushed a
drill chassis close to the wall — inch by inch to reduce the noise of
the high, iron wheels on the gravel and scattered artifacts of
Jorgesson's yard.

Jorgesson was lying on the floor by the door, or rather Jorgesson
was lying on a woman who was on the floor by the door. It was the
only space available; the one strip for the door to open and the
clients to stand amidst Jorgesson's plunder. Jorgesson and his love
seemed accustomed to the position, for without needing to look
behind her, the woman reached an arm to brace herself on the stack
of long life batteries, and Jorgesson's trousers hung conveniently on
the impressive tines of a wapiti head behind him.

The apparent irrationality of sex is a vast humour to the young.
Jorgesson had no electricity in his hut, and the low, angled light
from a small Tilly was unflattering: single tendons jerking behind
Jorgesson's great knees were picked out, and the wrinkles behind
his head, and how flat his back-side was in fact. Of the woman there
was little more than the one practical arm, and her toes, separate

and tumescent as facets in the Tilly light.

'He's doing her,' said Dusty. 'He really is.' His voice had qualities of awe and relief; as if after all the furtive talk, the innuendo, the chapter endings, the fade-outs, he was reassured that the act itself was not a myth. Jorgesson was doing it before his eyes. 'Jesus,' said Dusty.

'Yea,' said Hec.

Jorgesson was unaware of any need to prolong his performance for our education. He slipped to the side, cleverly angling one leg between a brass fire guard and a Welsh dresser. He drew a rug about his love, and laid his bare arm upon it to stroke her hair. A candle sheen seemed on his arm in the localised Tilly light, and his face was all Punch features as he talked, stark in relief and shadow. Braces were a limp bridle from the wapiti, and the love's toes had coalesced with the passing of ecstasy.

The Ace of Diamonds Gang found an aftermath of restful affection disappointing. Dusty grumbled on the drill perch, and Bernie began hand signals of obscure intrigue. We had come to punish Jorgesson, and his pleasure would provide another cause. We withdrew to the darkness of Jorgesson's open shed to plan our assault. 'Have you got the card?' said Bernie. It was my turn: my turn to spike it, as Bernie said. I could feel it in my top pocket.

They gave me two minutes to creep around to the front of Jorgesson's hut, and there I took the card from my pocket and the brass pin from the side of my shoe. As I fixed it to the centre of Jorgesson's door, fellow partisans began their attack: stones cascaded upon the roof, Ashley ran towards me down the flank of the hut banging the boards with a length of piping, Dusty and Hec gave their wolf howls, Bernie beat a scoured copper in sonorous rhythm. The Ace of Diamonds Gang had released its terror.

I could hear also a sudden commotion as Jorgesson tried to rise from amongst his possessions to counter-attack. I had joined the others in a race for the gate when Jorgesson seemed to smite down the door and was behind us, like a black jumping jack with profanity as his sparks. His voice was husky with passion, and rage gave him an initial impetus — but we were prepared. Fled; the white masks and red diamonds flowing in and out of colour as we raced past the street lights. We were our own audience, struck by the audacity of the Ace of Diamonds Gang; avengers, raiders, sentinels, even if Bernie had to carry his glasses as he ran and had trouble keeping up. 'Wait on, wait on,' he kept calling, which impaired our wraith-like progress.

Jorgesson gave up though, once we reached the Sherwood of the timber yard. It was darker amid the stacks and he had no intimate knowledge of the trails there. He halted and sent in a verbal pack of bastards, buggers and sods to harry us on our way.

'Go home shagger,' shouted Hec.

'Serve him right,' said Dusty, but his tone was one more of envy than impartial justice.

'Remember the Ace of Diamonds Gang,' called Bernie hauntingly. We joined thumbs on one of the stacks when Jorgesson was gone, and enjoyed the exaggeration of what we had done: except Hec, who had to go straight home and risk being belted.

The depleted Ace of Diamonds Gang maintained its identity through the streets and short cuts from the timber yard to its macrocarpa headquarters; each scout call an echoing clearance. Yet after victory over Jorgesson there was arrogance rather than caution in our progress, and in the macrocarpa, darker than the blue, summer night, we put aside our masks and our greater lives with unspoken dismay.

In my room I folded my mask and placed it within the fuselage of the Spitfire Mk II; the special place. I began to undress, and as I pulled my jersey over my head I could feel my library card still in the shirt pocket from the afternoon. Except that it wasn't the library card; it was the Ace of Diamonds sign made out of the back of a Xmas card, and as I recognised it there was a flux of all my stomach, and blood pumping up my eyeballs, hair follicles quickening all over my skin, falling electrical cadences of primeval terror through the matter of the brain. It was the library card I had pinned on the door of Jorgesson's army hut in the second-hand yard. The Ace of Diamonds Gang had witnessed his secret love, had interrupted it, had taunted him from the night sky and the timber stacks — and I had left my library card pinned to the centre of his door to avow responsibility.

I dreamt of Jorgesson's retribution during the night, starting up in abrupt horror at each climax revealed. Jorgesson in the Headmaster's study when I was sent for, Jorgesson waiting in the shadows with an old sickle from stock, Jorgesson fingering a garroting cord beneath the swaying pines, Jorgesson at the door with my library card and asking to see my father.

That's how it happened. I had just taken a mouthful of Toad in the Hole when I saw through the kitchen window an unnaturally tidy Jorgesson coming past the geraniums. There was a bulge in his pocket which could have been a garroting cord, and his Punch head was tilted to accommodate a paisley tie. I have always since hated geraniums and paisley patterns. A geranium is a coarse, disease ridden plant with a flare of animosity and paisley resembles a slide of pond water beneath a microscope. Even Toad in the Hole has never been quite the same again. My father and Jorgesson spent time in sombre conversation, and although I couldn't catch the words I could see on Jorgesson's face successive expressions of contained outrage, reasonableness, social duty to parents of evil children. My library card passed from Jorgesson to my father; the indisputable proof of a tale too rich to be denied.

My father punished me with the razor strop, and rang the parent of each friend I had unhesitatingly betrayed. It was the end of the Ace of Diamonds Gang. It was the end of wraith-like sorties into the consciousness of our town; it was the end of silhouettes upon the timber stacks, of thumbs clasped to pledge the redress of makeshift grievances. It was the end of free imagination, and of boyhood perhaps.

THE PHILOSOPHER

Uncle Blick was a philosopher. He didn't write any books or anything about his views, but he kept sifting the experiences and observations of his life until he had a fair understanding of human motive. My parents didn't think Uncle Blick was a philosopher, at least I never heard them call him one. He was my mother's brother and had married a girl with a good deal of money. My father habitually had a very rude way of expressing the means by which Uncle Blick got his money. I don't think my parents could ever really accept the ease with which he encompassed life; his scepticism was a threat to their view that life was serious and therefore important.

At the end of my second university year I received proof that Uncle Blick was a philosopher, when I visited him while waiting to hear how many units I had failed. They'd rented a beach house, and as well as Uncle Blick and Aunt Janice, there was her close friend, Mrs Ransumeen, a widow, and her son Rodney. Between young Rodney Ransumeen and Uncle Blick there existed an unspoken but recognised dislike, for Rodney had no soul and Uncle Blick as a philosopher had become expert at divining such people. Uncle Blick thought it probable that, like dogs, they could see only in black and white, although they had learnt to talk in terms of colour. The soulless were not restricted to any class or occupation, he said; they were found everywhere. They were the culmination of man's physical evolution; resourceful, active, ambitious, lacking only sympathy, which is imagination.

On the Thursday before I was to leave, my aunt and Mrs Ransumeen took the car and went in to the city for the morning. Rodney wanted to try fishing for spotties from the jetty and being a boy of irreproachable caution and trust, he was allowed to. Uncle Blick and I remained behind, sitting in the sun of the rented garden amid the floribunda roses. What happened that morning now appears preposterous, yet at the time in the company of Uncle Blick it seemed perfectly natural, even inevitable. The seduction of Uncle Blick's neighbour, Mrs Lemage, and her daughter Phyllis was accomplished kindly by Uncle Blick, with myself as a rather fatuous extra for much of the time. The verbal banter across the fence was charged with his rich, idiosyncratic and considerate wit: his invitation to sherry and fudge cake apparently irresistible. As they made their way from their house to ours Uncle Blick finished his chapter in Tacitus and carefully marked the place before closing the book. Gravely he presented me to mother and daughter, then fell in step with Mrs Lemage, marching through the clustered floribunda to the patio.

We were all in the living-room when Rodney came in. Uncle Blick the philosopher had Mrs Lemage cornered among the puce curtains at the window and was just patting her rump in a healthy if somewhat detached manner. The Lemages seemed a little embarrassed and left soon afterwards. Rodney withdrew to the kitchen and sat on the tall bar-stool cleaning his fish, scratching round their dull, plastic eyes and hard mouths.

Uncle Blick stood at the window gazing up the coast. 'Go and ask Rodney what he's going to do,' he said at last. For myself Rodney's decision meant little, but for my uncle the situation was more hazardous, for Aunt Janice had a suspicious mind at any time and had already ruled that the Lemages were 'not nice'.

Rodney looked up when I spoke to him, his face bright with righteousness.

'I'm telling,' he said with imperial finality.

'He's telling,' I told Uncle Blick. His reaction was not fear, anger or despair, but a sudden intellectual exhilaration; his heavy face seemed to tighten and his eyes to take on a steadfast concentration to meet the challenge thrust upon him.

'What is the time, Hugh?'

'About eleven.'

'We have an hour,' said the philosopher.

'They're bound to believe him.' Perhaps I said it a little vindictively, for like all weak people I was at times seized with resentment of my uncle's assurance.

'Exactly,' he said.

'I can't see any way of stopping him telling his mother and Aunt Janice what he saw. You know his peculiar integrity. He won't be bribed and we can hardly kill him.'

'To hurt or intimidate Rodney would be an admission of inferiority, as well as prone to failure. No, Rodney must discover the bitter essence of the adult world.' Uncle Blick's conversation often had such a solemn universality, as if, Gladstone-like, he addressed more listeners than could be seen. 'Rodney is honest, straightforward, articulate and intelligent.' Uncle Blick paused in admiration of the calibre of his enemy. 'He is also malicious. But the most significant thing is that Rodney is ten years old.' Here Uncle Blick broke off to prod me in the chest with a heavy finger. 'See? For a child, Hugh, a thing is true or false with strict logic; no such division exists in the adult mind, though it is often claimed. For us the distinction is between the credible and the incredible; the adult replaces logic with experience as the touchstone of reality. Strange that it is almost the reverse of what we like to believe concerning old and young. This world of difference between Rodney and his mother will provide escape. We must hide the truth in an unacceptable magnitude of truth.'

We began Uncle Blick's campaign by leap-frogging into the kitchen to gain Rodney's attention. Uncle Blick took off his shoes and anointed his feet in the sink from a carafe of burgundy before climbing out of the window and munching several gentian blooms growing beneath it. Rodney followed, missing nothing, saying nothing; an encyclopaedic observer. He watched while Uncle Blick clumsily scaled the flower trellis and stood on the tiles to urinate down the chimney; he watched while I took out the small wheelbarrow and ran over Uncle Blick's legs as he lay in the fresh lawn clippings by the glasshouse. Rodney saw it all, and when Uncle Blick and I returned from a wash and change, he was already in wait by the door as the womenfolk returned.

Like a dwarf ringmaster Rodney ushered in Mrs Ransumeen and my aunt and then adopting an accusing posture, he pointed at Uncle Blick. 'He had Mrs Lemage next door and that girl over here and he was touching her on the bottom because I saw him.'

My aunt said nothing, but the warmth in her face drained quickly away. Her hands opened, the long, slender fingers for a moment fully extended then slowly crumpling.

'Rubbish!' Uncle Blick smiled tolerantly from his chair.

'Rodney never lies,' said his mother, looking defensively at her oracle.

Rodney continued, his voice tremulous and urgent. 'He poured wine over his feet and he ate some of those blue flowers, and he climbed right up on to the roof, and he — you know — well, he piddled down the chimney.'

There was a long silence.

'You silly boy. I do hope you're not going to get one of those headaches again,' said Mrs Ransumeen in irritation.

'Too much sun,' said Uncle Blick kindly.

Rodney opened his mouth to speak, but instead he burst into tears. His mother took him out.

Uncle Blick picked up his pipe and drew its amber stem gently between his fingers. His face disclosed once more the lines of quiet resignation.

'An excellent exhibition, dear,' his wife was saying. 'A pity you missed it. Particularly the landscapes, so much less *informal* than in previous years.'

Uncle Blick the philosopher nodded. He gave me a brief smile and his hand sought out his Tacitus as he prepared to remove himself to a more spacious age.

KENNETH'S FRIEND

At the north side, towards the point, the shore was rocky. When the tide was going out I liked to search the pools for butterfish and flat crabs like cardboard cut-outs, sea snails with plates instead of heads, and flowing anemone in pink and mauve. Once Kenneth let a rock fall on my hand there on purpose, after I told him I didn't want to spend the morning making papier-mâché figures. He said it was an accident of course, but I knew he meant it. The rock had a hundred edges of old accretions, and cut like glass. I sat and waited for the sun to stop the cuts bleeding. I thought about Kenneth and me, and how I came to be there at all.

I had good friends when I lived in Palmerston North, friends that experience had shown the value of, but when we shifted to Blenheim I didn't have time to make friends before the holidays. I liked Robby Macdonald best. He and I became close later, but Kenneth seemed to attach himself to me in those first weeks. Perhaps he felt it gave him at least a temporary distinction to be seen with the new boy. He came home with me often after school, and lent me *Crimson Comet* magazines. At Christmas time he invited me to go with his family to their holiday home in the Queen Charlotte Sounds. His father was a lawyer and mayor of the town. My mother was pleased I'd been invited, and for sixteen days too. She gave me a crash course on table manners and guest etiquette. I had a ten-shilling note in an envelope, so that I could buy something for Kenneth's parents before I left.

The house had a full veranda along the front, facing out towards the bay. We used to have meals there, and standing out like violin music from amongst the talk of the Kinlethlys and their guests, I could hear the native birds in the bush, and the waves on the beach. It was a millionaire's setting in any country but ours, though Mr Kinlethly was a lawyer and mayor of the town admittedly. Glow-worms too; there were glow-worms under the cool bank of the stream. At night I crept out to see them, hanging my head over the bank, and with my arms in the creek to hold me up. The earth in the bush was soft and fibrous; I could plunge my hands into it without stubbing the fingers. The sand of the small bay was cream where it was dry, and yellow closer to the water. There was no driftwood, but sometimes after rough weather there would be corpses of bull kelp covered with flies, and filigree patterns of more fragile sea-weed pressed in the sand.

What Kenneth wanted, I found out, wasn't a friend, but someone to boss about. A sort of young brother, without the inconvenience of his sharing any parental affection. With no natural authority at school, Kenneth made the most of his position at the bay. Each night before we went to bed, Kenneth enjoyed the privilege of choosing his bunk and so underlined his superiority. He might bounce on the top bunk for a while, then say that he'd chosen the bottom one; he might wait until I'd put my pyjamas on one of them, then he'd toss my pyjamas off and say he'd decided to sleep there himself. He liked to play cards and Monopoly for hours on end, or work on his shell collection. Whenever we had a disagreement as to what we should do, Kenneth would say that I could go home if I didn't like it. I think in a way that's what Kenneth wanted — for me to say that I wanted to go home, that I couldn't stick it out. He didn't understand how much the bay offered me, despite its ownership. Kenneth's parents didn't know we disliked each other. We carried on our unequal struggle within the framework of their expectations. We slept together, and set off in the mornings to play together; we didn't kick each other at the table or sulk to disclose our feud. His parents were always there however, as a final recourse: the reason I had to come to heel and follow him back to the house when he saw fit, or help him catalogue his shells in the evening instead of watching the glow-worms.

The Kinlethlys seemed to take their bay for granted; corrupted by the ease and completeness of their ownership. Mr Kinlethly was away more days than he was there, and at night he shared the family enthusiasm for cards. I never saw him walk into the bush, and he went fishing only once or twice; a sort of tokenism. There was no doubt he was pleased with the place though; he liked visitors so that they could praise it, and I heard him telling Mrs Kinlethly that the property had appreciated seven hundred percent since he purchased it. Mrs Kinlethly had some reservations I think. She wouldn't allow any uncleaned fish near the house. She said the smell lingered. We would gut them at the shore, washing the soft flaps of their bellies in the salt water, and tossing their entrails to the gulls. Mrs Kinlethly gave us what she called the filleting board, and we would scale and dismember the blue cod and tarakihi in the ocean they came from; the filleting board between Kenneth and me, our feet stretching into the ripples. Mrs Kinlethly seemed sensitive to the smell of fish. When the wind was strong from the sea, blowing directly up to the house she said it smelled of fish. It didn't really. It carried the smell of kelp, sand-hoppers, mussels, jetty timber, island farms, distant horizons — and fish.

One wall of Kenneth's room was covered with the display case of his shells, and our bunks were the opposite side. I thought the collection interesting at first; the variety of colours and shapes, the neatly typed documentation. Each entry seemed to have one sentence beginning 'This specimen . . . ' Mr Kinlethly wrote them out, and Kenneth proudly typed them on the special stickers, which I got to lick. 'This specimen a particularly fine example from the northern coast of Sabah', 'This specimen a gift from Colonel L. S. Gilchrist following a visit to our bay' or 'This specimen one of the few examples with mantle intact'. The collection seemed to admirably satisfy the two Kinlethly requirements concerning possessions — display and investment.

My dislike of the shells began when I had sunstroke. Kenneth and I had been collecting limpets on the rocks, and I forgot to wear a hat. The sun on the back of my neck all morning was too much for me. I lay on the bottom bunk, and tried not to think of the bowl Mrs Kinlethly had placed on a towel by the bed. The family considered it rather inconsiderate of me to get sick. After all I was there to keep Kenneth amused, not to add to Mrs Kinlethly's workload. I lay there trying not to be a bother, and hearing Kenneth's laugh from the veranda. In the late afternoon Mr Kinlethly brought a guest back from Picton, and they came in to see the shells. 'A friend of Kenneth's' said Mr Kinlethly as my introduction. I was bereft of any more individual name at the bay. It was always 'Kenneth's friend'. 'I think he's been off colour today,' said Mr Kinlethly. 'Now here's one in

particular; the Cypraea argus.'
  'Oh yes.'
  'And Oliva cryptospira.'
  'Strikingly formed, isn't it?'
  'Cassis cornuta.'
I wanted to be sick. The nerves in my stomach trampolined, and saliva flooded my mouth. The mixing bowl on the towel seemed to blossom before me. Mr Kinlethly was in no hurry. 'Most in this other section were collected locally,' he said. 'Kenneth is a very assiduous collector, and also people around the Sounds have become aware of our interest. A surprising number of shells come as gifts.' Despite myself I looked over at the shells. Many of them seemed to have the sheen of new bone; like that revealed when you turn the flesh away from the shoulder or knuckle of a newly killed sheep. I had to discipline myself, so that I wasn't sick until Mr Kinlethly and his visitor had left the room. The shells were always different for me after that.

The Kinlethlys had a clinker-built dinghy. It always had a little bilge water in it that smelled of scales and bait. They had their own boatshed for it even; just like a garage, with folding doors so that the dinghy could be pulled in, and a hand-winch at the back of the shed to do it with. The dinghy was never put in the shed while I was there. Kenneth said they left it out all summer. We used to pull it up the sand a way, and then take out the anchor and punch one of the flukes in the ground in case of a storm or freak tide. Using the dinghy was probably the best thing of all. When we went fishing I could forget the boring times, like playing Monopoly, and helping Kenneth with his shells. I could look down the woven cord of the hand line, seeing how the refraction made it veer off into the green depths, and I could listen to the water slapping against the sides of the dinghy. Closer to shore the sea was so clear that I could see orange starfish on the bottom, and the sculptured sand-dunes there, the sweeping outlines formed by the currents and not the wind. Flounders hid there, so successfully that they didn't exist until they moved, and vanished again when they stopped as some magician's trick.

Wonderful things happened at the bay, even though I was only Kenneth's friend. Like the time we were out in the dinghy and it began to rain. The water was calm, but the cloud pressed lower and lower, squeezing out what air remained between it and the sea, and then the rain began. I'd never been at sea in rain before. The cloud dipped down into the sea, and the water lay smooth and malleable beneath the impact of the drops. The surface dimpled in the rain, and the darkest and closest of the clouds towed shadows which undulated like stingrays across the swell. 'I never think of it raining on the sea,' I said to Kenneth. 'Imagine it raining on whole oceans, and there's no-one there.'

'Bound to happen,' said Kenneth. He couldn't see why I was in no hurry to get back.

'I always think of it raining on trees, animals, the roofs of cars,' I said weakly. I couldn't share with Kenneth the wonder that I felt.

Kenneth had no respect for confidences. That evening at tea, when Mrs Kinlethly told the others how wet he and I had got in the dinghy, Kenneth said that I'd wanted to stay out and see the rain. 'He didn't know that rain fell on the sea as well as on the land,' said Kenneth. That wasn't the whole truth of it, but it was no use saying anything. I just blushed, and Mrs Kinlethly laughed. Kenneth's father said, 'Sounds as if we have a real landlubber in our midst,' in a tone which implied he wasn't a landlubber. I learnt not to talk to Kenneth about anything that mattered.

On the Thursday of the second week there were dolphins again at the entrance of the bay. I admired dolphins more than anything else. They seemed set on a wheel, the highest point of which just let them break the surface before curving down in the depths. I imagined they did a complete cart-wheel down there in the green water, then came sliding up again, like a side-show. 'There's dolphins out at the point,' said Mr Kinlethly. Mr and Mrs Thomson and their two unmarried daughters were with us on Thursday.

'I've never seen dolphins,' said Mrs Thomson.

'Quite a school of them,' said Mr Kinlethly. He decided that his guests must make an expedition in the dinghy to see the dolphins. Mrs Kinlethly wouldn't go, but the Thomsons settled the dinghy well down in the water and there wasn't room for both Kenneth and me.

'There's not enough room for both the boys,' said Mrs Kinlethly. Kenneth didn't care about the dolphins, but he wasn't going to let me go. He called out that he wanted to go, and his father hauled him aboard.

'Kenneth's friend can come another time,' said Mrs Thomson vacuously, and the dinghy pulled away clumsily. I waded out a bit, and kicked around in the water to show I didn't care, but I could see Kenneth with his head partly down watching me, waiting to catch my eye, and with the knowing little grin he had when he knew I was hurt. The dinghy angled away towards deeper water, the bow sweeping this way then that, with the uneven rowing of Mr Kinlethly and Mr Thomson.

'Dolphins, here we come,' I heard Kenneth shouting in his high voice.

That finished it for me; not missing out on the dolphins, but Kenneth going merely because he knew I wanted to. I'd taken a good deal, because after all I was just a friend of Kenneth's invited for part of the holidays, but I was beginning to think myself pretty spineless. I thought of my Palmerston friends, and the short work they'd have made of Kenneth. I left Mrs Kinlethly watching the dinghy leave the shelter of the bay to reach the dolphins at the point. I went up to the house; across the wide, wooden veranda and into Kenneth's room. From the bottom bunk I took a pillow case, and began to fill it with shells from Kenneth's collection. I tried to remember the ones he and his father liked best; the ones most often shown to visitors. Pecten maximus, Bursa bubo, and Cassis cornuta, the yellow helmet. The heavy specimens I threw into the bag, and heard them crunch into the shells already there. Once committed to it, the enormity of the crime gave it greater significance and release. Whatever outrage the Kinlethlys might feel, whatever recompense they might insist on, Kenneth would understand: he'd know why it was done, and what it represented in terms of him and me.

I took the shells up the track into the bush, and I sat above the glow-worm creek and threw the shells into the creek bed, and into the bush around it. Most disappeared without sound, swallowed up in the leaves and tobacco soil. The yellow helmet stuck in the cleft of a tree, and as I sat guiltily in the coolness, and heard the ocean in the bay, it didn't seem incongruous to me, that Cassis cornuta set like a jewel in the branches. The bush was a good imitation of an ocean floor, or so I could imagine it anyway.

A sense of drabness followed the excitement of rebellion. I came down to the house, and replaced the pillow case. Without a plan I began to return to the beach, scuffling in the stones and listening to the sound of the sea. Mrs Kinlethly came up the path towards me. I thought she must have found out about the shells already, and her response was more than anything I'd expected. She walked with her hands crossed on her chest, as if keeping something there from escaping, and her tongue hung half out of her mouth. I tried not to look at her face, and I felt the muscles of my arms and shoulders tighten, like at school just before I was strapped. Mrs Kinlethly passed so close to me that I heard the leather of her sandals squeaking, but she didn't stop or say anything. She went up the steps, and the house swallowed her up in complete silence. I couldn't work out what was happening. I sat down there by the path and waited. I looked out towards the bay and the drifting gulls, letting the wind bring the associations of the sea up to me.

Mr Kinlethly came up next; without his trousers and with everything else wet. Instead of his hair being combed across his head as usual, it hung down one side like ice-plant, and the true extent of his baldness was revealed. 'The dinghy went over. Kenneth's gone,' he shouted at me forcefully, and looked about for others to tell. He seemed amazed that there was just me by the path in the sun, and the birds calling in the bush behind the house. His eyes searched for the crowds that should have been there to receive such news. When I made no reply, he turned away despairingly. 'Kenneth's gone. I must get to the phone,' he shouted at the monkey-puzzle tree by the veranda, and he strode into the house. His coloured shirt stuck to his back, and on the ankle of one white leg were parallel cuts from the rocks.

The house filled rapidly after Mr Kinlethly made his phone calls, until there were enough people even for him: relatives from both sides of the family, friends, and folk from the next bay. Two policemen from Picton came; quiet men who kept out of the house, and began the search for Kenneth. I rang my father when I could, and asked him to pick me up at the turn off by four o'clock. My mother had made it very clear to me about thanking the Kinlethlys before I left, but the way it was I couldn't bring myself to say anything. I just packed my things, and walked up to the road to wait for my father. I was up there by mid-afternoon, and I climbed up the bank above the road and sat there waiting. I hadn't had anything to eat since breakfast. I could see right over the bay, and although the house was hidden by the foreshortened slope and the bush, I could see the boatshed like a garage at the edge of the sand. Where the dinghy had capsized at the point, the chop was visible, occasional small, white crests in the wind.

PRINCE VALIANT

There's some ugly country in New Zealand; don't let them tell you it's not so. Some of it is the country we are to form in our own image perhaps. The Sinclair property was part of it. Bush had been taken off the slopes years before, and the soil was slumping into the gullies; the outwash was spoiling what river flats there'd been. Eight and a half thousand hectares of land in an agony of transition. And Sinclair's place was only one of several just the same.

Sinclair had his priorities right. Money for super, then for his stock, then for his family. The country there just died without top-dressing every other year. It was no use asking for anything to be done about the shearers' quarters. Over the four seasons that I could remember, nothing had been improved. The wall above the stove was still blistered bare of paint from the oven fire we had in the first year I went. The bunks had only slats, and palliasses with a smell of mildew and string. Under the bottom bunk by the door was a pile of *National Geographic* magazines with the covers torn off. I could look up from the glossy artificiality of winter in Vermont, or West Irian religious rites, and see the scoured track to the yard. Dog kennels with the beaten ground to the extension of the chains, and a tide mark beyond each of a hundred mutton bones. The bones stuck from the ground like defective teeth. No-one ever came from the *National Geographic* to see it all, even when it was summer in Vermont.

I joined the others at Sinclair's. The gang didn't come up to full strength until well into the summer. I spent several months on forestry work at Dargaville, and started shearing again when they moved up country. Cathro still ran things. We had a fresh roustabout, but Neddy was the only new shearer. Neddy was younger than the rest of us: all elbows, knees, and eyes of level intensity if you bothered to notice. Neddy was a good shearer. Tall, so that he suffered in the back, but flowing in his style and with the ability to calm sheep with his grip. Top class shearers have that. Others, like Norman and Speel Harrison, transfer their impatience so the sheep will struggle if they can. I've seen Speel brain them with the handpiece when his temper was up.

Neddy wasn't disliked, and his shearing ability was recognised. He was easy and without malice. His laugh and brief replies were at once obliging and dismissive. He never drew close into the group. Perhaps it was his subtle lack of deference, or a companion's realization after a time with Neddy, that he considered one person very much like another and placed no great store on any; least of all himself.

Neddy was the one we called Prince Valiant, because of his car. It was a Chrysler Charger. He had it resprayed while they were working at the place before Sinclair's. A metallic green of gloss and iridescence. For some reason he'd never replaced the bumpers, and the brackets stuck out like small antlers at the charge. In scroll work on each side were the words Prince Valiant. The letters were chrome yellow with black edging, and a lance was the underline, piercing the letters.

So he was Prince Valiant you see. At times there was something of a sneer in its use. The car was thought a pretension by the Harrisons and Sinclair. Neddy didn't seem to mind. He spent a lot of time on his car. He had twin speakers mounted by the back window; and a line of clammy, little monsters hanging suspended there. They were green and purple, the colours of cloudy jellies. He had a file box in the front passenger's footwell, and he kept all his country and western tapes there. People like Willie Nelson and Whitey Schaeffer, Efram Nathan and Webb Pierce. Often during breaks, or after lunch, Neddy would go and sit in his car with the door open. He'd play his tapes, drink beer and gaze over Sinclair's raddled land.

Neddy talked to me only once about the car. I was sorting and oiling combs, and he was making himself new sack slippers. A few deft tucks, and some stitches with the bag needle. 'I like to drive,' he said. 'I like to drive at night. Close everything up, turn on the music, and drive. At night what's outside could be anywhere. It just falls away behind. The music and me in there driving. It's a whole world.' He looked at me quickly with intent eyes. The laugh he gave disparaged himself, lest my reply should do it. Neddy had been expelled from school. He couldn't get the hang of it, he told me. All the time he was at school Neddy felt he was getting pushed around, and having no sense of the existence of other people he couldn't see any reason for being pushed around. Neddy's family hadn't done much by him I gather. Cathro knew a bit about it. All I ever heard from Neddy was a comment in the shed when the Harrisons used the bale stencil to brand the roustabout's backside. He said his father had used a hot clothes iron on his mother.

Another thing which kept Neddy a bit apart was the intensity of his interest in a girl in Te Tarehi. It had been going on most of the summer, Cathro said. No matter where they were working, every second or third night Neddy went all the way down to Te Tarehi to see his girlfriend. He'd put on his blue slacks and stock boots after tea, and that would be the last of him until the Charger came rumbling back up the track. Norman and Speel complained about being woken up when Neddy came into the quarters late, so several times when Neddy had had more beer than usual, he just switched off the car, and slept right there. I've come out before breakfast and have seen him lying asleep, his polished stock boots dangling from his ankles, and his face pressed into the crease at the back of the seat.

Neddy's girlfriend was a source of undeclared envy. Speel and I resented being left with a pile of *National Geographics* without covers, and a monologue from his brother about the Social Credit philosophy. Speel tried to convince himself that Neddy's girlfriend in Te Tarehi wasn't worth it. He said he'd met someone who knew her: that she was flat-chested and the town bike. Neddy would carry on getting ready; waxing his stock boots, or taking his blue slacks from the newspaper underneath his palliasse. 'Bite your arse,' he'd say with a smile. The less Neddy said about his girl in Te Tarehi, the more desirable she became.

We were due to finish the last mob at Sinclair's on a Friday. On Thursday evening Neddy came out again ready for town. The ends of his hair were wet because he'd been cleaning his face. His blue slacks had pewter buttons on the back. In one hand he held three beer bottles by the necks like chickens. He laid them along the bench seat on the passenger's side. Sinclair had come down to catch him. 'You could do a job for me, Prince Valiant,' he said. Sinclair was pleased to demonstrate his familiarity with the joke. 'If you can get your mind off shagging that is.' Sinclair tried to take some paper from his trouser pocket, but the trousers were too tight, and the pocket opening was pressed flat. 'It's a note for the Wrightson's agent.' Sinclair squirmed and swore. 'You'll need to go to his house. The office will be shut.'

'I won't be going that way.'

'There's only one way to Te Tarehi, for god's sake!' Sinclair gave a burst of laughter, drawing the others into laughter too. Neddy made himself comfortable in his car. He switched on a tape. Sinclair had the folded sheet at last from his pocket. He came confidently towards Neddy's open window with it.

'Bite your arse,' said Neddy gently, and the Charger moved away. The misshapen creatures jiggled in the back window, the posts of the yard made a pattern of reflections in the green, metallic paint.

'Bastard,' said Sinclair. He went into the quarters to find Cathro and complain. 'Cathro, Cathro,' he called.

The Charger didn't come back during the night. Before we started next morning Cathro rang the two other homesteads in the district, in case Neddy had broken down, but they knew nothing. Then after ten, Mr Beaven rang back. Neddy's car had been seen in a gully on the Ypres Creek turn-off, and Neddy was dead.

Cathro and I drove up. Mr Beaven and his head shepherd were there. They were waiting for the constable from Te Tarehi. The car had missed the corner and struck the yellow creek bank. From the road there seemed to be no damage. The metallic paint was un-touched beneath the fine dust that the dew had set. But when we climbed down we found the Charger had struck with force. Mr Beaven and his man had covered Neddy and the dash with a rug from the back seat. His legs lay in a restful pose partly out of the door. I could see from the soles of his stock boots, how little wear they'd had. The flaccid monsters hanging in the back window jos-tled each other in the wind.

It was an intrusion to wait alongside the car. We went back up to the road and waited for the police. We leant on Mr Beaven's car and talked. 'He's been driving around here night after night,' said Mr Beaven. 'We keep seeing the lights from the homestead; along Kelly's Cut, the Through road, and here as well. We passed him on the road coming up at times. A green Chrysler without bumpers. He must have been covering a hundred miles or more a night, just cruising round.'

'Listening to his music,' said Cathro. 'Neddy loved to be by himself, listening to his music as he drove. The boys called him Prince Valiant.'

'I saw that on the car,' said Mr Beaven. 'All doo-dahed up all right.' Cathro didn't say anything about Neddy's girlfriend in town: the girl that each of us had imagined according to his own expectation, and who had no other life.

Those nights Neddy had left us, he'd fired up on beer and music, driving along the top roads. It didn't say much for our company, but then ugly country breeds ugly people I suppose. Even so, the death of someone you don't know well can have its acid, for without the protection of emotion there's a clarity in what is bleak and random. As we sat and waited in the morning, I thought of Neddy driving alone; with his dashlights, the monsters, the songs of Whitey Schaeffer and Webb Pierce. And in the darkness that poor country slipping by.

VALLEY DAY

Every second month Brian went with his father on the Big Kick. They drove up the valley and the minister took services at the little church of Hepburn and at the Sutherlands' house. One midday service at Hepburn going up, one in the afternoon at Sutherlands', then the evening drive home. In the autumn the long sun would squint down the valley and the shadows blossom from hedges and trees, and slant from the woodwork of buildings in angles no longer true.

One sermon did the trick on the Big Kick, with only the level of formality altered to suit the circumstances. The minister was relaxed despite the hours of driving, and treated it as a gallant expedition for his son's sake. 'Off on the Big Kick again, eh,' he said. 'The Big Kick.' The scent of the hot motor, taste of finest, stealthy dust, sight of the valley floor paddocks all odd shapes to fit the river flats; and higher in the gullies sloping back, the bush made a stand. Few farmhouses; fewer cars to be met, and dust ahead a clear warning anyway.

Brian had his hand in the airflow and used it to feel the lift on his palm. He assessed the road. Each dip, each trit-trotting bridge, places he would set his ambushes. Hurons or Assyrians swarmed out to test his courage, while his father practised parts of the sermon, or recited Burns and then murmured in wonderment at such genius. Brian made the air take some of the weight of his hand, and he kept his head from the window when a small swamp of rushes and flax was passed in case there were snipers hiding there.

'Will the one-armed man from the war be there?' he said.

'Mr Lascelles. Don't draw attention to it.'

'It happened in the war.'

'His tank was hit, I believe. The arm was amputated only after a long struggle to save it: not until he was back in New Zealand. I visited him in hospital I remember.'

'You can still feel your fingers when you've got no arm.' Brian said. 'They itch and that. If someone stood on where they would be then you'd feel the pain.'

'No,' said his father; but the boy kept thinking it. He saw a cloud a long way off like a loaf of bread, and the top spread more rapidly than the bottom and both were transformed into an octopus.

Hepburn was a district rather than a settlement. The cemetery was the largest piece of civic real estate, and the greatest gathering of population that could be mustered in one place. Mrs Patchett had nearly finished cleaning the church. She was upset because a bird had got in and made a mess, and then died in the pulpit. She said there were holes under the eaves. Even such a small church maintained its fragrance of old coats and old prayers, of repeated varnish and supplication, and insects as tenants with a life-cycle of their own. The air was heavy with patterns of the past: shapes almost visible, sounds brimming audible. An accumulated human presence; not threatening, instead embarrassed to be found still there, and having no place else to go. There were seven pews down one side, and six on the other. Down the aisle stretched two parallel brass carpet crimps, but no carpet in between. One stained window, all the rest were plain, a bloody poppy amidst green and blue, dedicated to the Lascelles brothers killed within three days of each other in the great war.

Brian took the bird out on the dust shovel. It left just a stain on the boards behind the pulpit. He threw the bird above the long grass: it broke apart in the air, and the boy closed his eyes lest some part of it fly back into his face. He brought his father's bible, soft and heavy, from the car, and the travelling communion tray with the rows of small glasses set like glass corks in the holes, and the bottle full of the shed blood of Christ.

'Don't wander off then,' said his father. 'Don't get dirty, or wander off. Remember we'll be going with one of the families for lunch.' The boy was watching a walnut tree which overshadowed the back of the church, and ranks of pines behind. He found a place where Indian-like he was hidden, but could look out. He crossed his legs and watched the families begin to arrive. The Hepburn church no longer had a piano, and the man with the piano accordion came

early to practise the hymns required. Rock of Ages, and Turn Back
O Man. He was shy, very muscular, and prefaced everything he
played or said with a conciliatory cough. Fourteen other people
came as the piano accordion played. Fourteen adults and six children. Brian watched the children linger in the sunlight before trail-
ing in behind their parents. The one-armed Mr Lascelles came. Even
to Brian Mr Lascelles didn't look old. He wasn't all that many years
back from the war, and he laughed and turned to other people by
the cars as if he were no different. Brian got up and walked about in
the pine needles as if he had only one arm. He looked back at the
trees he passed, and smiled as Mr Lascelles had done. Without
realizing it he walked with a limp, for he found it difficult to match a
gait to having one arm.

The accordionist coughed and began to play, the families sang,
and the boy stood still at the edge of the trees to see the valley and
bush on the hills. Rock of Ages cleft for me, let me hide myself in
thee. He felt a tremor almost of wonder, but not wonder, a sense of
significance and presence that comes to the young, and yet is neither
questioned by them nor given any name. All the people of that place
seemed shut in there singing, and he alone outside in the valley. He
could see all together the silvered snail tracks across the concrete
path, the road in pale snatches, the insect cases of pine needles
drawn immensely strong, the bird's wing in the long grass, the
glowing Lascelles poppy in the sunlit window. Rock of Ages cleft
for me. Brian tipped his head back to see the light through the pines
and the blood ran or the sky moved and the great, sweet pines
seemed to be falling, and he sat down dizzy, and with his shoulders
hunched for a moment against the impact of the trees. The church
was an ark with all on board; it dipped and rolled in the swell of the
accordion, and he alone was outside amidst the dry grass and
shadows, a sooty fantail, gravestones glimpsed through the falling
pines of his own life.

He saw cones. The old cones, puffed and half rotted in the
needles were ignored. He wanted those heavy with sap and seed,
brown yet tinged with green, and shaped as owls. When dislodged
they were well shaped to the hand to be hurled as owl grenades
against impossible odds across the road, or sent bouncing amongst
the gravestones to wake somebody there. He gathered new stocks
by climbing with a stick and striking them from the branches. At
first he climbed carefully to keep the gum from his clothes, but it

stuck to him anyway, gathered dirt and wouldn't rub away, and lay like birthmarks on his legs and held his fingers.

His father was preaching, for the church was quiet. Brian heaped up a mass of pine needles beneath the trees; working on his knees and bulldozing the needles with both hands out in front. He built a heap as high as himself, and jumped up and down on it. When he lost interest he left the trees and walked into the graveyard to search for skinks. Quietly he bent the grass from the tombstones, like parting a fleece, and after each movement he waited, poised in case of a lizard. He found none. He imagined that they were destroyed by things that came down from the bush at night. He picked at the resin stains on his hands. Deborah Lascelles, 1874-1932, Called Home. Brian forgot about the skinks. 'Called Home,' he said to himself. He thought about it as he went down the tree-lined margin of the small cemetery and on to the road. He was disappointed that there were no new cars, but one at least was a V8. He shaded his eyes by pressing his hands to the door glass, in an effort to see what the speedo went up to. He reasoned that anyway as it had twice as many cylinders as their car, it must do twice the speed.

Old now is Earth, and none may count her days. The final hymn. Brian went back into the trees and stood as king on his pine needle heap. He arced his urine in the broken sunlight as an act of territory, and checked the two balls in his pouch with brief curiosity. He jousted against the pines one more time, and brought down a perfect brown-green owl. He ran his hand over the tight ripples of his cone; he hefted it from hand to hand as he went back to the church.

His father stood at the doorway to shake hands and talk with the adults as they left. Those still inside showed no impatience. They talked amongst themselves, or listened with goodwill to what was said by and to the minister. There were few secrets, and no urgency to leave the only service for two months. Mrs Patchett showed Mr Jenkins the holes beneath the eaves, and he stuffed them with paper as an interim measure, and promised to return and do more another day. Things borrowed were transferred from car to car. Wheelan Lascelles stood unabashed, and on his one arm the white sleeve was brilliant against the tan. 'That poem you used,' he said to the minister. 'What poem was that?'

'One of my own in fact.' Brian shared his father's pleasure. They smiled together. The boy edged closer to his father so as to emphasize his affiliation.

'Is that so. I thought it a fine poem; a poem of our own country. I'd like some day to have a copy of it.'

From the sheets folded in his bible the minister took the hand-written poem, and gave it. It was found a matter of interest to those remaining: the minister giving his poem to Wheelan Lascelles. Others wished they had thought to mention it, and strove to recall it.

'We're going to the Jenkins' for lunch,' Brian's father told him when everyone had left the church. The Jenkins lived 20 kilometres up the valley. The minister preferred having lunch with a family living past the church, for then in the afternoon the trip to Sutherlands' was made that much shorter. He let the Jenkins drive on ahead because of the dust, and followed on. 'Mr and Mrs Jenkins eat well,' he said to his son with satisfaction.

On a terrace above the river were the house and sheds of the Jenkins' farm, and a long dirt track like a wagon trail leading in, and a gate to shut behind. 'What have you got on yourself?' said the minister as he checked appearances before entering the house.

'Gum.' Brian rubbed at it dutifully, but knew it wouldn't come off.

'And what's in your pocket?'

'Just a pine cone,' he said. His father flipped a hand as a sign, and Brian took the owl and rolled it away. It lay still warm from his body on the stones and earth of the yard.

'You realise old Mrs Patchett died of course and wasn't there today,' said Mrs Jenkins when they sat. Brian thought someday he might return and find his pine cone grown far above the Jenkins' home. 'Her mind went well before the end. She accused them of starving her, and used to hide food in her room. The smell was something awful at times.' Mr Jenkins smiled at Brian and skilfully worked the carving knife.

'She wasn't at the services the last time or two,' the minister said. 'I did visit her. As you say her mind seemed clouded, the old lady.' Mr Jenkins carved the hot mutton with strength and delicacy.

'She was a constant trial to them,' Mrs Jenkins said. Mr Jenkins balanced on balls of his feet, and gave his task full concentration. Like a violinist he swept the blade, and the meat folded away.

'I saw Mr Lascelles who's only got one arm,' said Brian.

'Yes, Wheelan Lascelles,' said Mr Jenkins without pausing.

'Old Mrs Patchett was a Lascelles,' said his wife. 'They only left her a short time, but she must have tried to walk back up to where the first house on the property used to be. She went through the bull paddock, and it charged you see. She wouldn't have known a thing of it though.' With his smile Mr Jenkins held the gravy boat in front of Brian, and when the boy smiled back, Mr Jenkins tipped gravy over his meat and potatoes and the gravy flowed and steamed.

'The second family in the valley were Patchetts,' said Mrs Jenkins, 'and then Lascelles. Strangely enough Wheelan's father lost an arm. There must be long odds against that I'd say. It happened in a pit sawing accident before Wheelan was born.' Brian stopped eating to consider the wonder of it: two generations of one-arm Lascelles. On the long sill of the Jenkins' kitchen window were tomatoes to ripen, and a fan of letters behind a broken clock. And he could see a large totara tree alone on the terrace above the river.

'And which was the first European family?' said the minister as he ate.

'McVies. McVies and then Patchetts were the first, and now all the McVies have gone one way or another. McVies were bushmen of course, not farmers, and once the mills stopped they moved on.'

'I haven't seen a McVie in the valley for thirty years,' said Mr Jenkins, as if the McVies were a threatened species, fading back before civilization.

'If your father has only one arm then you're more likely to have one arm yourself,' volunteered Brian.

'Play outside for a while,' his father said. 'Until Mr and Mrs Jenkins and I have finished our tea.'

'There's a boar's head at the back of the shed,' said Mr Jenkins. 'We're giving the beggars something of a hurry up recently.'

'There you are then,' said the minister.

The boar's head was a disappointment; lopsided on an outrigger of the shed. It resembled a badly sewn mask of rushes and canvas. False seams had appeared as if warped from inner decay. Only the tusks were adamant in malice; curved, stained yellow and black in the growth rings. Brian reached up and tried to pull out a tusk, but although the head creaked like a cane basket, the tusk held, and only a scattering of detritus came down. The vision of the bull that murdered old Mrs Patchett was stronger than the defeated head of a pig. The boy sat in the sun and imagined the old lady escaping back to her past, and the great bull coming to greet her.

'What happened to the bull?' he asked his father as the minister topped up the radiator.

'What's that?'

'What happened to the bull that killed Mrs Patchett?'

'I don't know. Why is it you're always fascinated with such things? I don't suppose the bull could be blamed for acting according to its nature.'

As they left amidst the benevolence of Mr Jenkins' smile, and the persistent information from his wife, Brian saw his cone lying in the yard: green and turning brown, and he lined it through the window with his finger for luck, and saw it sprout there and soar and ramify until like the beanstalk it reached the sky. 'A substantial meal,' said the minister.

'There was too much gravy,' said Brian.

'I was born in country like this,' said his father. The bush began to stand openly on the hillsides, and on the farmland closer to the road were stumps which gripped even in death. 'It's awkward country to farm,' said the minister. 'It looks better than it is.' There would be a hut in his pine, and a rope ladder which could be drawn up so that boars and bulls would be powerless below. Tinned food and bottles to collect the rain. Mr and Mrs Jenkins wouldn't realize that he was there, and at times he would come down to the lower world and take what he wanted. 'They tried to make it all dairy country, but it didn't work,' his father said. Brian was willing to be an apparent listener as they went up the valley; mile after mile pursued only by the dust.

Dogs barked them in to Sutherlands'. The Oliphants and more Patchetts were already waiting in the main room. There was a social ease amongst them, arisen from a closeness of lifestyle, proximity and religion. The Sutherlands had no children left at home; the last Patchett boy was at boarding school; only the Oliphant twins, six-year old girls, were there to represent youth. They sat with their legs stuck out rebelliously because they weren't allowed to thump the piano keys. The Sutherlands had a cousin staying who was a catholic. Brian watched him with interest. There was a mystery and power in catholicism he thought; a dimension beyond the home-spun non-conformism that he knew from the inside. Surely there was some additional and superstitious resource with which to enrich life. 'Absolutely riddled with cancer,' Brian heard Mr Oliphant tell the minister.

When the minister was ready the service in the living room began; there was no more exact timing necessary. Mrs Sutherland played the piano, and Mr Oliphant enjoyed singing very loudly and badly. The Oliphant twins refused to stand up with the adults, remaining in a sulk with their legs stiff before them. Their eyes followed Brian past the window as he went from the house. He thought the piano disappointing in comparison with the accordion; more inhibited and careful, less suited to the movements of leaves and water, to the accompaniment of birds.

Brian remembered a traction engine from previous visits. Once it had been used in the mills, but since left in the grass: heavy iron and brass, and great, ribbed wheels. It was warm from the sun, and Brian scaled it and sat there. The traction engine had been built to withstand enormous pressures, and before an age of planned obsolescence. It was a weathered outcrop; the rust only a film which didn't weaken, and the brass solid beneath the tarnish. A land train cast there amidst the barley grass and nodding thistle. He shifted what levers were not seized, and rocked to suggest the motion of the engine on the move.

'You get tired of all the services, I suppose?' said the Sutherlands' cousin. He stood in his carpet slippers, and wore a green woollen jersey despite the heat. He was almost bald, with just a rim of coarse, red hair, like the pine needles the boy had heaped up in the morning. Brian came down to talk. It seemed discourteous to remain raised up. 'I'm in charge of the afternoon tea. I'm a catholic, you see.' His eyes were deeply sunk, like the sockets of a Halloween pumpkin. 'I've nothing against your father.' They watched heavy, white geese trooping past the sheds. 'There's cake of course, but you know there's water-cress sandwiches as well. Can you imagine that.' Brian thought it rabbit food, but the cousin was from the city. 'She went and collected it from the creek, just like that. There's wonder still in the world,' he said. 'Did I tell you I'm a catholic?' The cousin began to cry without making any noise, but shedding tears. Brian gave him some privacy by taking a stick and beating a patch of nettles by the hen-run. But the cousin wiped his tears away and followed him. He didn't seem interested in maintaining an adult dignity any more. 'Is that gum on your legs?' he said. The boy told him that he had been playing in the trees at Hepburn.

'There's graves there. One said "Called Home" on it.'

' "Called Home", did it really.' The cousin shared Brian's fascination with the phrase. 'Called Home.' He began to laugh: not a social laugh, but a hoarse laugh, spreading downwards and out like a pool. A sound of irony and fear and submission.

Mr Oliphant began shouting 'Earth might be fair, and all men glad and wise.' The cousin listened with his mouth still shaped from the laughter.

'I'd better see to the afternoon tea,' he said. 'There are lesser rendezvous yet. I'll crib another water-cress sandwich if I can hold it down.'

'Peals forth in joy man's old undaunted cry,' they heard Mr Oliphant singing.

'These things are at the end of my life,' the cousin said, 'and the beginning of yours. I wonder if they seem any different for that.' The cousin turned back from the house after a few steps, and came past Brian. 'Jesus,' he said. 'I'm going to be sick again.' He rubbed the flat of his hands on the green wool of his jersey as if in preparation for a considerable task, and he walked towards the sheds. He gave a burp, or sudden sob.

The Sutherlands, Mr Oliphant and the minister came out in search of him when their afternoon tea wasn't ready. Brian could see the Oliphant twins looking through the window. 'Have you seen Mrs Sutherland's cousin?' Brian's father asked him. The boy told him about the crying and the sheds.

'I hate to think — in his state of mind,' said Mr Sutherland. He and the minister began to run. Mr Oliphant saw his contribution best made in a different talent. He filled his lungs. 'Ashley, Ashley,' he cried: so loud that birds flew from the open sheds, and the Oliphant twins pressed their faces to the window. The echoes had settled and Mrs Sutherland had prevented him from further shouting, when Mr Sutherland came back.

'It's all right,' said Mr Sutherland. 'He's been sick again that's all. He's got himself into a state.'

'Who can blame him,' said Mrs Sutherland.

'He was going to make the afternoon tea,' said Brian. 'He started to cry.'

'He's a good deal worse today, but the Rev. Willis is with him.' Mr Sutherland was both sympathetic and matter of fact. 'They're best left alone,' he said. 'Come on back to the house.' Mr Oliphant was disappointed that it wasn't the end; not even a more dramatic approach to the end.

'A sad business,' he said in his lowest voice which carried barely fifty metres. Brian was left to wait for his father. He thought that in that quiet afternoon he could hear Ashley's sobs and his father's voice. He climbed back on to the throne which was the engine, and rested his face and arms on the warm metal.

A column of one-armed Lascelles was moving back up the valley from the war, each with a poem in his hand, and the accordion played Rock of Ages as they marched. Mr Jenkins deftly knifed a wild pig, all the while with a benevolent smile, and in his torrent voice Mr Oliphant Called Home a weeping Ashley: deep eyes and woollen jersey. A host of pine owls, jersey green and brown, spread their wings at last, while old Mrs Patchett escaped again and accused her kin of starvation as she sought an earlier home. Behind and beyond the sway of the accordion's music, and growing louder, was the sound of the grand, poppy-red bull cantering with its head down from the top of the valley towards them all.

HAMMOND'S STAND

Time winnows our experience in a quite unconscious way, and looking back we are surprised at the significance some things have once the trivia is gone. I'm thinking of Hammond and his school fees.

Education is free, compulsory and secular; but everything in a democracy is a matter of degree. Our school had fees for extra things like cricket pads, cyclostyled sheets dealing with the intestines of fish, and subsidised buses to the museum. The Hammond family claimed they shouldn't have to pay for their education: the school considered that the quality of its instruction could be maintained only with the financial involvement of parents. Both were right. Truth is often ambiguous when well-intentioned people disagree.

Our form master was Stamford Hall. He never had a nickname because the boys found out he hated to be called Stamford. So Stamford he always was. He said Stamford Hall made him sound like an institution, or a family seat. Stamford Hall was renowned for meticulous administration; not much of a teacher actually because he lacked the patience to explain things. But he was a very well-organized man. Nobody missed Stamford Hall's classes, for he never failed to have a roll-call, and he never failed to follow up an absentee no matter how long he had to wait. He counted out the strokes when he caned, lest he should give more or less than a just measure.

Collecting the school fees was something Stamford Hall never shirked. He gave a reminder on Wednesdays, and signed receipts in the form period on Fridays. His signature was thick and grandiose, like that of an institution.

When the first deadline for payment of fees passed, Stamford

Hall would read out the names of defaulters on a Friday, and finally he wrote on the board the names of those few left. Dougherty, Crabb, Brown and Hammond — unpaid school fees. He put a red box around the names after two weeks; by then Crabb had paid and there were only Dougherty, Brown and Hammond. The next week he put an asterisk by the names of Dougherty and Hammond, and rubbed out Brown who paid all his five dollars in copper coins. The following Friday he didn't say anything about the fees at all, but he took first Dougherty and then Hammond by the ear, and led them up to the board. He made them stand on a chair, and by tugging on their ears aligned their eyes with the names on the chalk box. Dougherty's head was so close that he got some of the red chalk on his nose, and he walked back to his desk with the tip of his nose powdered like a billiard cue. Stamford Hall never said a word to either of them. The class enjoyed it. A little ritual humiliation is good for the soul; of the spectators in particular.

Dougherty cracked, and stole enough money from milk bottles to pay the fee. He'd spent the original five dollars on games at the arcade. He got back at Stamford Hall by scratching the bonnet of his car. It was a necessary act to maintain his self-esteem.

Hammond stood up the next Friday, when his was the only name left in the red box, and said that his parents refused to pay the school fees because education in our society is free, compulsory and sexualar. Stamford Hall enjoyed having a good line for the staff room so much that he forgot about fees for that day. A week later Stamford Hall said he was going to ring Hammond's parents if the money wasn't paid in three days. Hammond said that he and his family refused to pay on principle. Stamford Hall did ring, but Hammond's father was a communist and a tree doctor. Hammond said his father told Stamford Hall that he was eager to take the issue to court; failing that he was willing to meet Stamford Hall behind the gasworks.

It was Stamford Hall's turn to feel some pressure. He'd told Hammond that by the end of the term it had to be all settled. He talked with the Headmaster, and came back with something called the hardship clause to explain to Hammond. Stamford Hall told Hammond to check out the hardship clause at home, and then discuss it with him in private. Hammond stood up the next day and said that it was no hardship for his family to pay the fee, and he himself had one hundred and seventy-two dollars from holiday earnings, but that on principle there'd be no payment. Hammond said his father told him that paying school fees was only papering over the cracks in the system, and that teachers were the dupes of the system just as much as the pupils or parents. Hammond's father was a sound Marxist, though not great on imagery. He told his son that the capitalistic edifice was ripe for plucking.

Hammond's stubborn defence impressed the class. Some of us felt shame at having paid up so readily. Dougherty and Brown said they wanted their money back. Dougherty told Stamford Hall that his father was virtually a communist because he belonged to the boilermakers' union, and that therefore he wanted his money back. Stamford Hall caned him the next day for taking screws out of the furniture.

For the sake of administrative symmetry Stamford Hall offered to pay the money himself, but Hammond refused that charity also. The red box remained in the top corner of the blackboard, and in it, Hammond — unpaid school fees. It remained there for the rest of the year; not finally as any recrimination against Hammond, but as an expression of principle. Even Stamford Hall could see that finally. And Hammond never presumed upon his success. The chalk became smudged and faint, but when the relief teacher accidentally rubbed it off, Stamford Hall put it back again, clear as you like, red box and all. He'd played some passable rugby in his day had Stamford Hall, and he wasn't all bad. He proved he had a sense of history and could recognise an epic stand on principle when he saw one.

Hammond failed school certificate in everything but Technical Drawing. He left school to be in charge of the wire trolleys at the Tip-Top supermarket. He would give us the thumbs up as we passed, and we would do the same, grin, and wonder what other challenges he would withstand.

THE PAPER PARCEL

For a long time I thought everybody could see the future in the way I could myself: an expectation based upon desire. The dream logic of the mind. Even though events were often very different, it was the reality I blamed and not the vision. The reality failed to match the vision which was the first and greater view. The actual encroached, but expectation drew off, and set up again upon the high ground of the future.

I remember asking Dusty Rhodes what he thought being in a submarine was like. I dunno he said, I dunno do I, until I've been in one. What a way to live. He didn't know any better. He was spared any disillusion at least. No matter how many times it happened I felt a sense of loss and betrayal when things proved other than I had seen them. Not different only, but also less in fitness and in unity.

Like the fancy dress ball for instance. I was twelve when the senior classes had a fancy dress ball to end the year. It was a strict convention that you had to have a partner in advance. Anyone not paired off would hold his hand in fire rather than turn up that night. As far as I knew I had only three attributes to attract the opposite sex. I was the second fastest runner in the school, I was top in maths, and I had blue eyes. Dusty Rhodes was fastest boy. I never beat him, although sometimes I dreamt I might. I became accustomed to despair and his greasy hair in front of me as we ran race after race. Dusty drowned in the Wairau the next year; by the berth of the coaster which used to come over from Wellington and up the river. For years I had a guilt that I might have wished it. I was second fastest in the school to Dusty. I used to boast to the others that my legs just went that fast without any effort from the rest of me. To enhance this I had the habit of looking sideways as I ran, as if to see the cars on the road to the bridge, and escape the boredom of my automatic legs. Being top of maths was the second thing, and quite beyond my control. I was always top and never had an explanation for it. I was fearful I would lose the trick of it. And the blue eyes. There were only four boys with blue eyes in the class, and Fiona McCartney told Bodger that she liked blue eyes best. The class had been singing beautiful, beautiful brown eyes, and Bodger asked her which she preferred. Fiona McCartney blushed and said blue eyes, and the other girls giggled. I didn't forget that. I was beginning to store up points of knowledge about girls. Fiona McCartney was the oracle about such things at that school.

So those were the advantages I had going for me, and I exploited them to the full in the weeks before the fancy dress dance. I never ran so often or so fast; I was closer to first and further from third than ever before. I turned my head to the side with casual indifference and the old legs went with a will. I took to answering more maths questions in class, and fluked most of them right, and I used to widen my eyes when I was close to girls so that the blue of them would be more conspicuous.

Fiona McCartney passed a message to me saying she wanted to see me by the canteen at playtime, and when she came we went over by the sycamores and railing. She put one hand on the railing and swung her right foot in an arc on the grass. She glanced at her friends by the canteen and considered she had set a good scene. I widened my eyes at her, and held my breath without realizing it. She told me that she wouldn't be going to the dance with me. I hadn't asked her, but she knew she was every boy's choice and was letting me down gently. As I was the second fastest and so on she realized my expectations. I felt dizzy then remembered to breathe out again. She said I'd have no trouble getting someone to go with. The girls had been talking, she said. She said the girls had been talking, and she put the tip of her tongue between her teeth and smiled. I smiled back and widened my eyes, as if I were aware of what girls said.

It made me more anxious though, Fiona saying that, especially when we started having dancing practices. I wondered which of the girls had partners arranged already, for I wanted to avoid the humiliation of asking them. Kelly Howick saved me the trouble. At the third practice she said to me that I wasn't much of a dancer and was I going to the fancy dress night. I said that I thought that I probably would. Casually I said it, and looked to the side as if I were running. I widened my eyes too; which wasn't much good when I was looking away. Are you listening, she said. In the past I'd thought about Kelly mainly as the girl most likely to keep me from fluking top in maths. She was top in most things. She had definite breasts though, and was pretty. Only a certain matter-of-fact manner prevented her from being more like Fiona McCartney. It came to me that she was willing to be my partner. Only later did it also occur to me that she and her friends had made the decision without my presence being required. I will be your partner if you like, she said. She didn't need an answer. She seemed pleased for me. She smiled at me, and at her friends, as we moved awkwardly to the dancing instructions of Bodger and Miss Erikson.

I'd had my share of success in life, but in that school hall I felt for the first time the heady stuff of sexual preferment. Kelly Howick had sought me out. I looked with contempt upon the others in the hall. Dusty Rhodes who could only run fast, and Bodger with the sweat stains on his shirt. For the first time I perceived myself in the mirror of the feminine eye; I was filled with casual arrogance and power. I was aware of a new dimension to life. My head kept nodding indolently as we danced, and my shoulders shrugging in some instinctive male response.

The knowledge of sexual magnetism was a novelty. I felt I should be able to tap it for other purposes. The day after the dancing practice I raced Dusty again. I felt the new power within me and was resolved to express it in my running also. I would bury him. In fact it made not an inch of difference. I still had to run behind Dusty, his hair bobbing. And he didn't even have a partner to the dance. It was a shock to discover that the power generated by sexual preferment was not directly transferable to athletic performance.

In my mind I was quite sure how the fancy dress dance would be. Sure, I had been let down somewhat in the past by the failure of events to conform with my directions, but I wasn't responsible for that. I saw Kelly and myself always in the centre of the hall; always in the better light, and somehow slightly larger than our classmates. I would dance, or stand quietly and attract the attention of other girls because of my blue eyes and a certain calmness of manner. Kelly would be constantly asking my opinion, and I would be giving it with easy finality. Instead of the lucky spot waltz there would be quizzes on tables, or a sprint the length of the hall and back when Dusty happened to be outside.

Kelly Howick talked to me during practices. I made the adult discovery that some people are ugly. I'd had the foolish idea that there were no common standards of appearance. Now I began to realize otherwise. Collie Richardson for example, who told the best jokes in the school. He had a very small upper lip. It was like a little skirt, and his gums and teeth were always exposed beneath it. Once I realized he was ugly I never liked his jokes as much again.

At practices Kelly took over my instruction. She gave an individual repetition of what Bodger and Miss Erikson kept saying. You've not got much rhythm have you, she said. Me! Second fastest and with automatic legs. In other circumstances it would have irritated me, but in the complacency of preferment I let it pass. Certain things about girls have to be tolerated for the overall benefit.

I skidded on loose stones by the sycamores next day and put a long graze along my left forearm. Mrs Hamil put iodine on it and Kelly was quite concerned. It won't show on the night will it, she said. What are you going to wear anyway? What is your outfit like? Her saying that made my arm begin to throb. The blood seeped out into beads despite the iodine. I hadn't done anything about a costume. Getting a partner as the priority had obscured all other aspects of the dance. I asked my mother about it that night, and she said that's nice, a costume party is nice. Sure, we'll think of something. And my father made jokes for his own amusement about being cloaked in ignorance, or dressed in a little brief authority. I could tell they didn't have the right view of the ball at all; that they were thinking of it as some party, some kids' thing.

Tony Poole said his parents were hiring a full cowboy outfit with sheepskin chaps, bandanna and matched revolvers. Dusty's parents were pretty poor; I thought he wouldn't have much to wear even when he did arrange a partner. But he said his cousin had a Captain Marvel costume which had been professionally made. What is it you're going as, Kelly asked me again. I started questioning my mother once more. What was she going to do for me? Kelly was going as Bo Peep. What about my costume, I said to my mother. Oh, we'll rustle up something don't you worry, she said. But I did. The more casual and unperturbed she was, the more I worried.

Finally my mother said she thought I should go as a parcel. A parcel; Jesus. She remembered someone at the New Year's party as a parcel, and he was a great hit. It was a cheap costume too, she said.

A parcel; Jesus. It was the originality of it that intrigued her, she said. Anyone could go as a policeman or a musketeer, people grew tired of seeing them. The parcel left only head and limbs out she said, and I could make up a giant stamp with crayons; and over my parcel body have stickers saying Fragile, London, This Side Up, Luxemburg, Handle with Care. The parcel was set to torpedo my night with Kelly Howick. Bo Peep Kelly with her beginning breasts and braided hair, and me as a brown paper parcel with a stamp done in crayon.

There was a sense of inevitability about the parcel. I tried to persuade my mother that I should go as something else. I said I wouldn't wear it, but the parcel became part of me before I ever saw it; something irrevocable and humiliating before I was even dressed in it.

The dance was supposed to start at eight. It said so on the printed sheet I brought home. Nobody arrives at a dance on time though, my mother said. She never realized how little adult convention applies to the young. It said eight o'clock on the sheet didn't it? Why would it say that if it didn't mean it? Nobody comes to a dance till later, my mother said. It's just how it's done. But I saw eight o'clock written. I knew everyone would be there. Anthony Poole in his cowboy outfit, and Kelly as Bo Peep.

On that Friday I didn't run well. Dusty beat me without hardly trying, and although I looked away as I ran, I was having a hard time to keep ahead of Ricky Ransumeen in third place. My automatic legs were being affected. I thought a good deal about that because it seemed unfair. When I was selected by Kelly, when desirability was conferred on me, although the power was great it hadn't made me any faster, as I told you. But on that last day as I turned my head in studied casualness, instead of the flowing leaves of the sycamores by the fence, I saw myself in a parcel costume with a crayon stamp. Just for a moment there in the stippled leaves and keeping pace with me was a *doppelgänger* in a parcel. I lacked rhythm as I ran; I lacked a full chest of air; my automatic legs made demands.

It wasn't until after tea that my mother even began the parcel. I had to wear my swimming togs so no clothes would show below the parcel. The brown paper strips were wrapped around me like nappies, and round and round my chest, and a hole cut for my head and arms. I was tied with twine and with a yellow ribbon in a bow at the front. Over my heart was stuck the crayoned stamp, huge and serrated. Other oblong stickers were plastered on with flour-and-water paste. This Side Up, Handle with Care, On Her Majesty's Service, Do Not Rattle. I was finally packed by eight o'clock, and set off on my bike for the school assembly hall. I tried to sit up straight on the seat so that the parcel wouldn't crinkle too much. The wrapping made noises as I rode, and the greasy blue and red head on the stamp grinned in the setting sun. I told myself that the parcel was really quite clever and would go down well. I could only half believe it, yet I never seriously thought about not going. The power of sexual preferment was enough to transform me; it would make difference distinction, and nonconformity audacity. To be with Kelly Howick would be sufficient to defeat the parcel.

They had started of course. I knew it. The sheet had said eight o'clock after all. The light from the hall spilled out into the soft summer evening. The noise of the band and the dancing slid out with the light, and echoed in the quad. Bodger patrolled the grounds, alert for vandalism or lust. Late, said Bodger. He looked at my costume and said no more. As I went in he was still there on the edge of the light and the noise, and with the blue evening as a backdrop. He had his hands behind his back, and he swayed forward on his toes. Hurry up then, said Bodger. I slipped in round the edge of the door, and worked my way over to the boys' side. Tony Poole had a curled stetson, sheepskin chaps, check shirt and six-guns with matching handles. He came back from seeing Fiona McCartney to her seat. Tommy was a fire chief with a crested helmet that glittered, and a hatchet at his belt. Dusty's Captain Marvel insignia was startling on his chest, and his cloak was cherry rich and heavy. And I was a parcel. A brown paper parcel with bare legs and sandshoes. A brown paper parcel which crinkled when I moved. A brown paper parcel with a stamp drawn up in red and blue. It wasn't right: not for the second fastest runner in the whole school, not for the top maths boy, and the one preferred by Kelly Howick. What the hell is that you're wearing, said Dusty. Wouldn't you like to know, I said.

I went over to claim Kelly when the music began for the next dance. It was a foxtrot. I had learnt both sorts of dance. A waltz was where you took one step to the side every now and again, and a quickstep was where you kept forging ahead. A foxtrot is just a slower quickstep. I'm a little late, I said, smiling and nodding. I found without meaning to that I was trying to compensate for being a parcel. Kelly's Bo Peep outfit suited her. The bodice with the crossed straps accentuated her breasts, and she had a curved crook. She looked fifteen at least. As we danced I knew that she was looking at the parcel. I heard myself laughing loudly at Captain Marvel who was fighting with a pirate, but Kelly kept looking at my costume. I was going to come as a pirate myself, I said, I had a better pirate outfit than that; a huge hat with skull and cross-bones, and an eye-patch. What, she said. I was going to come as a pirate, I said. I can't hear you for all the noise your brown paper makes, Kelly said. It wasn't so of course. The band was making more noise than the parcel. No, she was giving me the message. Even the way she danced with me was different from the other times. She had a dull expression on her face, as if she was doing me a favour by dancing. I tried whirling her around, the way Bodger and Miss Erikson had demonstrated. I nearly fell over, she said. It was a lesson for me in the transience of sexual preferment. It was apparently something that had to be taken advantage of immediately.

I was determined not to mention being a parcel. Not admitting it was some way of keeping the full force of its humiliation from me. I quite like Dusty's Captain Marvel suit, I told Kelly. A bit overdone, but I quite like it. I told Miss Erikson I'd help with supper, she said. It won't be worth you coming over for the next dance for I'll start helping her soon I think. Sure, sure I said, we must have the grub on time. The grub on time! I couldn't believe I was saying it. And afterwards I'll probably help with the washing up, Kelly said.

Flour-and-water paste isn't very successful when there's any movement. Some of the stickers were starting to work loose on the brown paper. This Way Up fell on the dance floor. Handle with Care came off and I tucked it under the twine. It worked down low on my waist, and Dusty and Ricky Ransumeen started pointing and laughing at its anatomical juxtaposition. I took Kelly back to her side of the hall after the dance. See you then, I said. She slipped amongst the other girls with a murmur. Who could blame her? As I went back over the floor I could see several of my labels lying there. Fragile, Via Antwerp, Airmail. Maybe someone would start collecting them and draw attention to them. The parcel was ceasing to be recognizable as such. Without stickers, wrinkled and lopsided after the dancing, it had lost what little illusion of costume it ever had. I was a kid wrapped in brown paper and wearing bathing togs and sandshoes. Ah, Jesus me. Only the stamp over my heart seemed firmly stuck. A mark of Cain in crayon that leered out on all the world, and would not release itself or me. I was beaten all right. I couldn't maintain any longer my vision of how the night should be. And the withdrawal of sexual preferment had weakened me; my esteem had eroded. I began to work my way towards the door; a paper parcel through the batmen, policemen, riverboat gamblers and Indian chiefs. Little Wade Stewart was a Pluto. He came to me with Fragile. Is this yours, he said kindly. Yes, what a dag isn't it, I said. I kept moving towards the door, and reached it as the lucky spot waltz was announced.

It felt good outside. The summer dusk, the distanced and impersonal buildings, the lucky spot music fading as I made my way to the bikesheds. Bodger loomed up. I got a bit of a nosebleed, I told him, but as I was by myself he wasn't interested. I rode out of the grounds, and the crinkle of the parcel and the lessening music conjoined down the quiet street. I allowed myself the indulgence of self-pity for a time. I was outside myself; I accompanied myself; I consoled myself, for the bland incomprehension of adults and the loss of sexual status. I felt I had been hard done by, that was the truth. Perhaps there would be a fire in the hall. I imagined the flames leaping from the walls, and the riverboat gamblers and the fairy queens put to flight. Faster and faster I biked. I saw the fiery press of the blaze, the terror of my classmates, the impatience of Bodger and Miss Erikson. I stood up on the pedals in the soft, summer night and put on a sprint that would have carried me clear of any possible pursuit. Parcel my arse, I shouted, and louder, parcel my arse. I reckoned that I was about the fastest bike rider at that school. I reckoned that even Dusty Rhodes wouldn't be a patch on me at that. I felt the wind on my flight pushing the brown paper against me as I swept without a light down the blue streets.

There was a light in the living room when I reached home however. I put my bike away, and looked through the gap between curtain edge and window-side. My mother was listening to the radio and talking; my father was cleaning his shoes on a newspaper spread by his chair. I had to find some immediate focus for revenge, and they would serve as enemies. I crept into the kitchen and took a packet of my father's cigarettes from behind the clock, and struck a match to inspect the pantry cupboard. Mixed fruit pack, I chose; raisins, candied peel, sultanas, figs, cherries. I took the fruit pack and cigarettes to the woodshed. I sat on the pine slabs in the lean-to there, and ate the fruit mix and smoked my father's Pall Mall. I ripped off the stamp in crayon, and burnt holes in it. I flashed the glowing cigarette against the navy sky, writing Zorro in swift neon. I undid the twine and unwrapped the parcel, burying the pieces in the woodheap. Jesus, I said, so what? Who cares about the dance and being a paper parcel? I was still second fastest in the school wasn't I. Wasn't I! I sat in my togs and singlet, ate my dried fruit, and watched the smoke curl as shadows from my fingers. And next time it would be different. I could see so clearly the next year's dance; when I would be Napoleon and Fiona McCartney my Josephine. That's how it would be all right.

MR VAN GOGH

When he went into hospital our newspaper said that Mr Van Gogh's name was Frank Reprieve Wilcox, and that was the first time I'd ever heard the name. But I knew Mr Van Gogh well enough. He came around the town sometimes on Sunday afternoons, and he would excuse himself for disturbing you and ask if there were any coloured bottles to carry on the work of Mr Vincent Van Gogh. Whether you gave him bottles or not, it was better never to enquire about his art; for he would stand by any back door on a Sunday afternoon and talk of Van Gogh until the tears ran down his face, and his gaberdine coat flapped in agitation.

Only those who wanted to mock him, encouraged him to talk. Like Mr Souness next door who had some relatives from Auckland staying when Mr Van Gogh came, and got him going as a local turn to entertain the visitors. 'Was he any good though, this Van Gogh bugger?' Mr Souness said, nudging a relative, and, 'But he was barmy wasn't he? Admit it. He was another mad artist.' Mr Van Gogh never realized that there was no interest, only cruelty, behind such questions. He talked of the religious insight of Van Gogh's painting at Arles, and his genius in colour symbolism. He laughed and cried as he explained to Mr Souness's relations the loyalty of brother Theo, and the prescience of the critic Aurier. They were sufficiently impressed to ask Mr Van Gogh whether they could see his ears for a moment. Mr Souness and his relations stood around Mr Van Gogh, and laughed so loud when it was said, that I went away from the fence without watching any more. Mr Van Gogh was standing before the laughter with his arms outstretched like a cross, and talking all the more urgently. Something about cypresses and the hills of Provence.

Mr Van Gogh had a war pension, and lived in a wooden bunga-low right beside the bridge. The original colours of the house had given up their differences, and weathered stoically to an integration of rust and exposed wood. The iron on the roof was stained with rust, and look much the same as the corrugated weatherboards. The garden was full of docks and fennel. It had two crab apples trees which we didn't bother to rob.

Mr Van Gogh didn't appear to have anything worth stealing. He used to paint in oils my father said, but it was expensive and nothing ever sold, so he began to work in glass. No-one saw any of his art work, but sometimes when he came round on Sundays, he'd have a set of drinking glasses made out of wine bottles, or an ash tray to sell made out of a vinegar flagon. My father was surprised that they were no better than any other do it yourself product.

Although he had no proper job, Mr Van Gogh worked as though the day of judgement was upon him. He used his attached wash-house as a studio, and on fine days he'd sit in the doorway to get the sun. There he'd cut and grind and polish away at the glass. He would even eat in the doorway of the wash-house as he worked. He must have taken in a deal of glass dust in his sandwiches. Often I could see him as I went down to the river. If I called out to him, he'd say, 'Good on you,' still working on the glass; grinding, cutting, polishing. If I was by myself I'd watch a while sometimes before going down to the river. One piece after another; none of them bigger than a thumb nail. A sheet of glass sheds the light he said. They had to be small to concentrate the light. Some of the bits were thick and faceted, others so delicate he would hold them to the sun to check. Mr Van Gogh liked to talk of individual paintings as he worked — the poet's garden, street in Auvers, or starry night. He stored the different colours and shapes in cardboard boxes that said Hard Jubes on the sides. Yellow was difficult, the colour of personal expression, Mr Van Gogh said, but so difficult to get right in glass. He bought yellow glass from Austria, but he'd never matched Van Gogh's yellow. He never thought so much of his yellow glass he said, even from Austria.

Mr Van Gogh wasn't all that odd looking. Sure he had old-fashioned clothes — galoshes in winter and his gaberdine coat with concealed button holes, and in summer his policemen and firemen braces over grey work shirts. But he was clean, and clean shaven. His hair was long though, and grey like his shirts. He combed it back from his face with his fingers, so that it settled in tresses, giving him the look of a careworn lion.

Because my father was a parson it was thought he should be responsible for Mr Van Gogh and other weird people. Mr Souness said that it was just as well that my father had something to occupy his time for the other six days of the week. Ministers get some odd people to deal with I'd say. Reggie Kane was a peeping tom who had fits whether he saw anything or not, and Miss O'Conner was convinced that someone was trying to burn down her house at night, and she used to work in the vegetable garden in her night-dress. Our family knew Mr Van Gogh wasn't like the others, though most people treated him the same. My father said that Mr Van Gogh's only problem was that he'd made a commitment to some-thing which other people couldn't understand. My father had a good deal of fellow-feeling for Mr Van Gogh in some ways. Mr Van Gogh would've been all right if his obsession had been with politics or horse-racing. He wouldn't have been a crack-pot then.

Two or three times Mr Van Gogh came to our house to use the phone. He'd stand quietly at the door, and make his apologies for coming to use the phone. He was ordering more yellow glass from Austria perhaps, or checking on his pension. Mr Van Gogh's humil-ity was complete on anything but art. He was submissive even to the least deserving. On art though he would have argued with Lucifer, for it was his necessity and power. It was what he was. His head would rise with his voice. He would rake back his grey hair, and for a moment the backward pressure would rejuvenate his face before the lines could appear again; the plumes of hair being ҫ faint cascade upon his forehead. He could be derisive and curt, fervent and eloquent; but people didn't understand. A naked intensity of belief is an obscene exposure in ordinary conversation. It was better not to start him off, my mother said.

When the Council decided to make the bridge a two lane one, Mr Van Gogh's house had to come down. The engineers said that the approaches to the new bridge would have to be at least twice the width of the bridge itself, and Mr Van Gogh's house was right next to the old bridge. Even the house next to Mr Van Gogh's would probably have to go, the consultant thought. Mr Van Gogh took it badly. He stuck up the backs of the letters the Council wrote, and sent them back. He wouldn't let anyone inside to value the house; he wouldn't talk about compensation. My father said he was willing to try and explain the business, but he didn't know if he could justify it. The Council didn't seem to recognize the distinction.

As far as I know Mr Van Gogh never let anyone into his house. Even my father had to stand on the doorstep, and Mr Van Gogh stood just inside the door, and there was a blanket hanging across the hall behind him; to block off the sight of anything to a visitor at the door. My mother said she could imagine the squalor of it behind the blanket. An old man living alone like that she said.

My father did his best. So did the council and the Ministry of Works I suppose. They selected two other houses to show Mr Van Gogh, and a retirement villa in the grounds of the combined Churches' eventide home, but he wouldn't go to see them. He became furtive and worried. He'd hardly leave his house lest the people come and demolish it while he was away. The Council gave Mr Van Gogh until the end of March to move out of his home. Progress couldn't be obstructed indefinitely they said. Mr Souness looked forward to some final confrontation. 'The old bugger is holding up the democratic wishes of the town,' he said. He thought everyone had been far too soft on Mr Van Gogh.

In the end it worked out pretty well for the Council people. Mrs Witham rang our house at tea time to say she'd seen Mr Van Gogh crawling from the wash-house into his front door, and that he must be drunk. My father and I went down to the bridge, and found Mr Van Gogh lying on his back in the hallway, puffing and blowing as he tried to breathe. 'It's all right now,' said my father to Mr Van Gogh. What a place he was in though. For through that worn, chapped doorway, and past the blanket, was the art and homage of Mr Van Gogh. Except for the floor, all the surfaces of the passage and lounge were the glass inlays of a Van Gogh vision. Some glass was set in like nuggets, winking as jewelled eyes from a pit. Other pieces were lenses set behind or before similarly delicate sections of different colours to give complexity of toning. The glass interior of Mr Van Gogh's home was an interplay of light and colour that flamed in green, and yellow, and Prussian blue, in the evening sun across the river bank. Some of the great paintings were there: Red Vineyard, Little Pear Tree, View of Arles with Irises, each reproduced in tireless, faithful hues one way or another.

Mr Van Gogh lay like clay in the passage, almost at the lounge door. I thought that I was looking at a dying man. I blamed all that glass dust that he'd been taking in for years, but my father said it was something more sudden. He pulled down the blanket from the hall, and put it over Mr Van Gogh to keep him warm, then went down the path to ring the ambulance. The blanket hid Mr Van Gogh's workshirt and firemen's braces, but he didn't look much warmer. His face was the colour of a plucked chicken, with just a few small veins high on his cheeks. Very small, twisted veins, that looked as if they didn't lead anywhere. I stood there beside him, and looked at his work on the walls. The yellow sun seemed to shine particularly on the long wall of the lounge where Mr Van Gogh had his own tribute to the man we knew him as. In green glass cubes was built up the lettering of one of the master's beliefs — Just as we take the train to Tarascon or Rouen, we take death to reach a star — and above that Mr Van Gogh's train to Tarascon and a star rose up the entire wall. The cab was blue; and sparks of pure vermilion flew away. It all bore no more relation to the dross of glasses and ash trays that Mr Van Gogh brought round on Sundays, than the husk of the chrysalis to the risen butterfly.

My father came back and waited with me in the summer evening. 'It has taken years to do, years to do,' he said. 'So many pieces of glass.' The fire and life upon the walls and ceiling defied Mr Van Gogh's drained face. He'd spent all those years doing it, and it didn't help him. It rose like phoenix in its own flame, and he wasn't part of it any more; but lay on his back and tried to breathe. All the colour, and purpose, and vision of Mr Van Gogh had gone out of himself and was there on the walls about us.

Both the St John's men were fat. I thought at the time how unusual it was. You don't get many fat St John's men. They put an oxygen mask on Mr Van Gogh, and we all lifted him onto the stretcher. Even they stood for a few seconds; amazed by the stained glass. 'Christ Almighty,' said one of them. They took Mr Van Gogh away on a trolley stretcher very close to the ground.

'What do you think?' asked my father.

'He won't necessarily die,' said the St John's man. He sounded defensive. 'He's breathing okay now.'

Mr Van Gogh went into intensive care. The hospital said that he was holding his own; but Mr Souness said he wouldn't come out. He said that it was his ticker; that his ticker was about to give up on him. Anyway there was nothing to stop the Council and the Ministry of Works from going ahead. People came from all over the town to see Mr Van Gogh's house before they pulled it down. There was talk of keeping one or two of the pictures, and the mayor had his photograph in the paper, standing beside the train to Tarascon and a star. But the novelty soon passed, and the glass was all stuck directly to the walls with tile glue. The Town Clerk said there were no funds available to preserve any of it, and it was only glass anyway, he said. Someone left the door unlocked, and Rainbow Johnston and his friends got in and smashed a lot of the pictures. Mr Van Gogh's nephew came from Feilding, and took away the power tools.

My father and I went down to the river to see the house demolished. With Mr Van Gogh's neighbours, Mr Souness, and the linesmen who had disconnected the power, we waited for it to come down. There were quite a few children too. The contractor had loosened it structurally, and then the dozer was put through it. The dozer driver's mate wore a football jersey and sandshoes. He kept us back on the road. Mr Van Gogh's place collapsed stubbornly, and without any dramatic noise, as if it were made of fabric rather than timber. The old walls stretched and tore. Only once did my father and I get a glimpse of Mr Van Gogh's work beneath the weathered hide of the house. Part of the passage rose sheer from the wreckage for a moment; like a face card from a worn deck. All the glass in all its patterns spangled and glistened in yellow, red and green. Just that one projection that's all, like the vivid, hot intestines of the old house, and then the stringy walls encompassed the panel again; and stretched and tore. The house collapsed like an old elephant in the drought, surrounded by so many enemies.

'Down she comes,' cried the driver's mate, and the driver raised his thumb and winked. There was a lot of dust, and people backed away. Mr Souness kept laughing, and rubbed his knuckles into his left eye because of the dust.

'All the time Mr Van Gogh spent,' I said to my father. 'All that colour; all that glass.'

THE GIVING UP PARTY

Once the Jewells' place had been set in the countryside, but the suburbs had caught up with it, and dreary villas were camped around it. Apart from the house itself only the long drive from the road, and the front garden, remained from the days of elegance. The drive possessed a seemly curve, and was shadowed with a line of birches which kept down weed growth on the compacted earth and gravel. A weeping elm dominated the garden; vast, diaphanous, like a green fountain when stirred by the wind. The house had a tiled entrance hall, and lead-light windows with red and patterned glass facing the drive. The roughcast was of a texture Hugh never saw again; as if cream had been poured over marbles. On the hottest days the roughcast seemed ready to melt right off the house, and there were patches under the eaves and window frames where it had done so.

Hugh's father said the Jewells used to have their money in shipping, but lost a lot of it for being under-insured. Mrs Jewell had no husband. He had drowned years before while surf-casting. Hugh's father said he was renowned as a local stick man. It was some time before Hugh disassociated that comment from the fishing.

Each Saturday morning Hugh would bike out to the Jewells', turning off through the stone gate posts to pedal over the compacted drive beneath the birch trees. In winter his jobs were to cut kindling and fill the coal bins; in summer to mow the lawns. Mrs Jewell suffered from no vagueness, either aristocratic or induced by age. She would check the boxes of kindling by shaking them vigorously, and if the level dropped Hugh had to cut more. In summer she checked the lawns, with special attention given to the edges. She believed firmly that edges make a lawn. She would tour the lawns with Hugh, and her term of greatest satisfaction was adequate. Adequate became in Hugh's vocabulary a superlative. 'The lawns and edges are quite adequate, Hugh. Thank you,' Mrs Jewell might say on his good days.

Mrs Jewell's deft understatement was in keeping with her position. The rest of the town disliked the concept of position, without understanding it. People of importance, people of appointment, people of achievements; these are explicable in the scheme of things, but English born Mrs Jewell and her assumption of Position stirred a vague, post-colonial unease. The uneasiness was relieved by stressing the diminution of the family's wealth, and the reputation of her dead husband as a stick man.

Hugh was brought into the kitchen at the conclusion of each Saturday morning, given tomato or cheese sandwiches and a glass of cordial. Mrs Jewell always remained to see him eat; as if she feared he might blow his nose on the curtains, or start sharpening his teeth on the Welsh dresser. She would accompany him out to his bicycle, unless the weather was very cold, and give him his half-crown. He would feel the size and sheen of it; the solidness of it. Sometimes she would even hold his palm with one dry, firm hand while she gave him the coin, in case the responsibility of receiving it was too much for him. She thought of him as fifteen always; as he was when he first came to the house.

Mrs Jewell was economical of emotion; only the dogs seemed to really arouse her. They came from the surrounding sections, drawn by the spaciousness, the trees, the expanses of turned earth in the spring. Hugh rarely saw them, but Rankin did. He came in to keep the gardens on Friday and Saturday. Rankin said that during the week, when neither he nor Hugh was there, the dogs besieged Mrs Jewell. Rankin said Mrs Jewell had wept tears of rage and despair when she found the dogs had scratched the heart out of her gazania and laid their wastes there. They left white and yellow bones on the steps, they gambolled on the shadowed drive, and pissed on every vertical plane. Mrs Jewell pronounced the word dogs rather like ducks, and with chilling inflexion. She had a slug gun sent out from England, and she retaliated with it. Rankin showed Hugh the gun one morning. It was unlike the feeble guns sold locally, and fired heavy-weight slugs, not bee-bees. Rankin said that he had disinherited many a dog with it, and that Mrs Jewell would fire it herself. Rankin said with admiration that she always fired at the head.

All the winter mornings he worked at Mrs Jewell's seemed compressed in Hugh's mind to unremarkable routine, but the summer memories expanded as did the season which began them. And then it was a summer Saturday when he met Mrs Jewell's daughter, and that one day enlarged the sum of all others. It was the day of the junior representative cricket trials. The magnolia was out, and its flowers of carved soap lay amid new leaves that had undersides like a furred tongue.

'Magnolias tend to sulk,' said Rankin. 'They'll sulk for years sometimes before they choose to flower. A very feminine flower is magnolia.' Hugh stopped mowing one of the walkways to listen to him. 'And don't put any more clippings on the new compost,' said Rankin. He reminded Hugh that a depth of clippings generated too much heat, and as an after-thought he said that Mrs Jewell's daughter was home from England.

Rankin went on past, into the shrubs and trees of the garden. Hugh pushed back the grass in the catcher, and saw Mrs Jewell's daughter standing outside the front door, watching, with her hands in two big pockets in front of her skirt. She was wearing a vee-necked jersey like a boy's, with the sleeves pulled up, and sandals with heels. Her beauty took hold of Hugh and rattled his head until he gripped the mower for support.

'You're Hugh,' she said when she had come across the lawn. She said it as a stated introduction, not a question. 'I'm Helen Jewell. My mother told me that you'd be helping this morning. I'm to look after you, and you're to look after me.' She added the last to diminish the patronising sound of her mother's instruction. She pushed her hands into the exaggerated pockets of her skirt, and stared at the heaped grass in the catcher. 'We should have a motor-mower really, for the amount of lawn.'

'Your mother doesn't like the noise.'

'Noise is not genteel.' There was both affection and mockery.

'They are noisy though, and I don't mind the hand mower. Anyway if you had a motor-mower Mr Rankin would probably do the lawns himself, and there'd be no job for me.'

'I imagine that my mother likes to feel that she is employing two people,' said Helen. They stood in the sun; Helen looking at the garden. 'My mother thinks of this place as being somehow representative of England.' Hugh looked too, although he had no way of making the same comparison: the tulip plots, the lawns, the elm, the shrubs and birches along the drive. The direct heat of the sun seemed to deaden the sound of Rankin's whistling as he worked out of sight in the far corner of the garden. 'I lived in Wolverhampton when I was over there. I don't see England as a large cottage garden.'

'My mother thinks these are the nicest shrubs and trees in the town. She says that it takes over sixty years to have a garden like this.'

'It seems smaller. Not just the cliche of returning to a child's world, but rather that things have grown up so much. We used to have a tennis court on the lawn by the drive, and now with the elm and birches you can barely walk between them.'

'I've never seen a bigger elm than that.'

She went through one of the gaps in the tumbling leaves and branches, and Hugh was drawn after her. 'It's so much cooler in here; like inside a church.'

'Or a waterfall,' he said.

'It's odd you say that. My father's family had a struggle to get it started. They had to keep carting water to it for years he said.' The wind stirred the skirts of the weeping elm, and the lowest leaves swept patches on the ground worn clear of grass. All that water lavished on its growth; and now as if returning from the soil a cascade in the hot sun. The cooler air beneath the elm encouraged them to breathe more deeply, and the scents of the garden were more pronounced: the cut grass, magnolia, camellia, and the elm itself giving a subtle essence in its transpiration. 'The perfumed garden,' said Helen. She lifted her bare arms, and pushed them through the elm leaves. 'I can feel the sun on them outside,' she said. Hugh half extended his own arms, and then saw his hands were stained from the clippings, and dropped them quickly. Helen breathed noisily again. 'Isn't it terrible to drink in the morning,' she said. Hugh just smiled at the ambiguity. 'I feel that wine is more forgiving though. I wouldn't drink spirits before midday.'

'No,' said Hugh. He didn't care what she said. He just wanted her to keep lifting her brown arms, and smiling at him in the dappled light through the elm.

'But I'm holding you up,' she said. Some of the lawn close to the house still wasn't done.

'I've plenty of time,' said Hugh.

'No. You go on; get it done, then come into the sun porch and talk to me. I'm drinking alone. I'm having a party for myself this morning. A party, but no celebration.'

'I don't know the sun porch.'

'That one.' Helen moved to one of the openings in the elm, and pointed to the windows of the side entrance. Hugh watched her go back to the house. The heels on her sandals made her legs more shapely by raising the calf-muscle.

As he completed the lawn Hugh was in view of the windows of the house. Common sense told him that Helen wouldn't bother to watch him move round and round the lawn, but he was briefly self-conscious all the same. The awkwardness returned when he went to the sun porch. It was forgotten when she spoke. 'You've finished,' she said warmly; with a mixture of admiration and pleasure that from some women is the reward for even small achievements. 'I'm drinking wine,' she said, and raised her glass. 'White wine doesn't give me a head. It's my birthday after all, so I've started early.' Hugh tasted the wine she gave him. It was very different from that at his sister's wedding.

'How physical a thing is the sun on one's skin,' said Helen. She pulled her skirt up her thighs a way so more of her legs were in the sun, and she leant back in the chair, and turned her face towards the heat. She was not tanned, but her skin was naturally the colour of a dark hen's egg; brown and even, with the hint of inner warmth. Her arm with the glass showed no freckle or blemish, just warm egg-brown, and with a round bone in her wrist startlingly raised. Hugh sat on the window seat, and waited with his quiet smile. His bleached hair was heavy and straight. 'I'm sweating,' said Helen. Beneath the jersey she had no blouse, and she lifted it completely without affectation, and blew on to her chest and stomach. 'And the wine's getting warm. It's not really a good enough riesling to be drunk warm. Chilling hides faults in a wine.' She poured herself more however, tilting the bottle so much that the wine boiled in the glass and onto the floor. 'Oh damn,' she said.

'I'm thirty-four. I could be your mother, I'm thirty-four. Good god. Yet I look at you and feel that I'm your age, no more.'

'I'm older than you think,' said Hugh generously.

'I'm thirty-four, I'm a poet, and I'm back to living in my mother's house.' Her hair swung over her face, and she gave a shudder which cast it away. 'Do you read poetry?' He didn't, but more than anything he wanted to be able to recite something sensitive and perceptive there before her. All he could think of was a classroom poem; about a highwayman that came riding, riding up to the old inn door. So he said nothing, and traced with his finger on the window seat the shifting half-shadows from the elm fountain on the lawn. 'This can be my giving up party,' she said. 'You see? Like coming out, only far more significant.'

'It sounds a sad sort of party,' he said.

'I'm feeling sorry for myself today, and when you're feeling sorry for yourself you rarely have any pity for anyone else. Have you noticed that? I'm about to give up what's been central to my life; not poetry, but the idea that poetry could be the most important thing. That poetry could sustain my life; be sufficient to do that.'

'But you're beautiful.' He said it almost without sentiment: stated it simply and directly as an undisputed asset. Both knew that although it didn't seem to follow logically or immediately from what she'd said, yet it was relevant to what she meant.

'Do you think I am?' she said.

'Yes.' His throat was tight with the discipline required in saying it only once. He wanted to go on, until the insistence of repetition overcame the banality of the word.

'That can be the trap you see, for a woman. It means that there's always another option. No matter what the commitment to my work, I've always known that the fail-safe was there. Men could become more, and poetry less. Marriage even. A solicitor perhaps, or the right farmer. My mother has a list of them. Tonight she'll have some of them to the house for my birthday. I think one's flying from as far as Wellington.'

Hugh had never considered poetry as anything that a modern person would do all the time. His small impression of poetry was that it was unfailingly something produced at great remove from any place or people that he knew. 'Have you always been a poet,' he said.

'At school and university I was mad on netball. Spent hours practising it, and made top teams. I find it hard to imagine it now.' Hugh found it easy enough; the suppleness and co-ordination remained in everything she did. 'Maybe when I'm married, or whatever, the time of my life spent on my work will seem just as strange. I'm living my life and it's not enough.' She looked deliberately out on to the wonder of her mother's garden: the soap blossoms of the magnolia were caught by the sun against the green of the shrubbery. 'And it's not enough,' she repeated.

Hugh looked out too, his eyes unfocused, allowing the movements of the elm to dominate. Then he noticed the dog. It pushed out from the shrubbery, and stood half-exposed on the lawn. Its drooping face had a mixture of effrontery and fear. 'There's a dog in the garden. Your mother hates dogs.'

'Where?' Helen Jewell left the chair, and took her wine to the window.

'An ugly looking brown thing, like a labrador cross.'

'Brindled,' she said, and giggled.

'What?'

'It amuses me that it's brindled. It's a literary convention that all brindled creatures must be ugly and unpleasant. I can think of no greater horror for my mother than a brindled dog in her garden.'

'We could get the slug-gun,' said Hugh.

'Slug-gun?'

'Slug-gun. Your mother keeps it in the wash-house for the dogs.' Helen laughed again.

'Get it! Get it!' she cried.

Hugh brought the gun, and loaded it by the window. 'Quick,' said Helen, 'before it disappears.' The dog seemed to hear her, and its flabby jowls shook as it looked about. Hugh aimed for its stomach, where there wasn't much hair, and they could hear the smack of slug as it struck. The dog stood still for a moment, a look of perplexed agony on its face, then abruptly turned and disappeared back into the shrubbery. 'Incident is everything,' said Helen. 'I love incident in life without a moral.' She came from the window, and knelt on the floor. She rested one hand on the chair. The waist band of her jersey folded on the arch of her hips. Her smooth knees were perfect amputations, and slightly angled in a vee.

Hugh put the slug-gun away, and sat on the floor too, by the window seat. Helen seemed already to have forgotten the humour of the dog. She was drinking again. 'You're very brown,' she said. 'One of the things I liked about the whites in South Africa was how brown and fit they were.'

'I'm outside a good deal of the time.' Hugh wanted to tell her that he was in the cricket trials this afternoon. He thought he should be able to work it in naturally with the point about being brown, but the opportunity passed before he could phrase it in his mind.

'There's an irony in the situation as regards my work,' she said.

She ran a finger back and forth beneath her left breast, the wool whispering. Hugh imagined himself doing it; traversing her jersey there below the weight and curvature of her breast. As he imagined it he trailed his fingers slowly on the polished floor, in the flickering visual cadence of the elm tree's pale shadows. 'I know others have realized it. Any extreme position has dangers. We complain of the drudgery of earning a living, and blame that for stifling creativity. I thought I was one of the lucky ones there, for I could spend any amount of time on my work. Yet in the end my poetry was becoming too inward; drying up, trivialised. I looked out of flats in Stoke Newington or Wolverhampton, and was cut off from the vitality that comes from working with people, from belonging. You can see that?' There was urgency in her question, but she looked into her wine glass rather than at Hugh.

'People are what matter,' he said. 'I can see that. I suppose you can't reach them through poetry or anything else unless you know them. Watching people isn't the same as living with them.' It was his most daring contribution.

'Right,' she said. 'It's the things we do most that determine what we are in the end.' She bit her lips as she thought. It was the one mannerism which betrayed any agitation. Her mouth moved, and she delicately sought shreds of skin with her front teeth.

'I hope I'm not drunk before lunch. My mother's having people tonight for my birthday. A dinner for my giving up party. I don't drink during the day; certainly not morning. That's when I work. That's when the muse comes.' She looked out at the splendour of the garden in the sun: the tonings, shapes, the movement and the texture. 'This must be the most difficult country in the world in which to maintain a creative resolve. Nothing much of mine gets published here,' she said. 'Here it is expected that I write poems about being a woman, having an intuitive view of relationships, and all that bilge. I hate the word poetess.' She was quiet for a while, looking down and moving her fingers over the rim of her wine glass; then she raised her head and looked steadily at Hugh. 'It's like the disillusionment of a marriage,' she said. 'I chose poetry as my husband and I've found out that it can't give me everything. It's not enough for the whole of my life; the length and breadth of it. And I'm thirty-four; now I'm thirty-four.'

'You could always keep writing poetry as well as do other things. Combine it with getting married, or some job you like.'

'No, that's a difference in kind not degree. No, I don't think so.'

'Maybe a fresh start will bring new enthusiasm. You said your-self that you needed to be involved with people in the things that mattered to them. You said about being on the outside looking in, when you were in England.'

'Maybe.' She smiled at him, cheered by his admiration and the youthfulness of his bleached hair.

They heard Mrs Jewell's car in the drive, and saw the blue of it flickering through the birches as it approached the house. Hugh went and sat on the window seat. He glanced around the room, as if it were strewn with signs which might incriminate him. But out-wardly there was only the wine and the glasses. And Helen kneel-ing on the floor. There is always a certain wantonness in an excess of beauty. 'Mother's home,' she said; not with any apprehension, but matter-of-factly as if it marked the end of one thing and the begin-ning of another. The end of the giving up party, and the beginning of different priorities.

Mrs Jewell called out in her piercing, English voice, and when Helen answered, Mrs Jewell followed the sound, and came to the sun porch. She showed no surprise to see Hugh sitting on the window seat, and her daughter on the floor. 'Good morning, Hugh,' she said, and carried on to talk to her daughter. Yet her alert, bird-like eyes regarded him; noting his heavy, bleached hair, the size of his brown forearms, and a certain calmness in the way he sat there. Mrs Jewell wouldn't give Hugh cordial in the kitchen again, or press the half-crown into his hand in quite the same way. She didn't mention money, or the lawns, at all with her daughter there. She took up the two wine bottles and glasses, and bore them signifi-cantly away without comment. Helen made a quick child's face of mock contrition behind her back.

'I'll have to go,' said Hugh. They went out past the kitchen, and Hugh stopped in the doorway to say goodbye to Mrs Jewell.

'I'll see you next Saturday as usual Hugh,' she said. It served to remind him that the order of things had not altogether changed.

At the side trellis, by his bike, Helen shook back her hair. 'I've been down this morning,' she said. 'Really down, and you've helped me. A giving up party is bound to be sad, but sharing it is better. Sharing the time of it, even if not the reason of it.'

'I've enjoyed it.' They listened to the bumble bees clumsily as-saulting the rhododendron blooms behind the trellis, and Rankin's persistent and invisible whistle as he worked beyond the drive.

'I think I'll go up to Wellington for a while,' Helen said.

'Maybe you won't give up after all. Maybe in Wellington it'll be different.'

She placed her hands on his waist, and kissed him with increasing fullness. She leant back, and as the arch increased in her throat her eyelids closed. It was a kiss and embrace of circular passion; from her to him and back again. Through him almost: in a definite farewell to her own youth, and the commitment of youth. Hugh could smell the riesling, some faint scent, the egg-brown warmth of her skin, and the comfortable fragrance of her woollen jersey in the sun. His hands moved down her arms, and he lightly held her wrists in which the bones were startlingly raised. When she had kissed him she said, 'You are the only person, the only person who came to my giving up party, and I thank you for it.'

'I'll always remember it,' said Hugh, as she went back past the trellis towards the door. He stood with his bike for a moment, thinking about the morning, letting it settle in his mind. He could hear Helen begin to talk to her mother.

'Mother,' she said, 'I'm thirty-four today, and it gives me no joy. Who do you think I should marry?'

Rankin was waiting in the trees at the turn of the drive. He whistled and waved Hugh down. Hugh leant his bike on the scoured bark of a birch tree, and followed Rankin through the shrubbery to the corner of the garden where he was working. Rankin thought it his right to gossip about his employer, but he had an artisan's pride which made him continue his work while he did so. With practised ease he cleared one nostril by blocking the other with his thumb and blowing, then he began digging out another barrow of compost. 'What did she talk about then?' he demanded.

'Her poetry mainly, and so on.'

'She's been here most of the week I gather,' said Rankin. 'Yesterday she was in shorts. I can't get on with my work. It's not good at my age.' He fragmented the compost in the barrow with two particularly powerful blows. Hugh smiled and watched the great elm waltzing above the lesser trees of the drive. He had established few certainties to guide him in seventeen years, but he knew enough to be naturally protective of anything beautiful; even the experience of beauty. 'You can't remember a damn thing about what she said,' Rankin accused Hugh. 'With a woman like that nobody can. You just soak her up. Am I right then?'

He was right about not remembering so much of the things she said, while acute in recollection of her presence. As Hugh looked away from Rankin, into the garden, he could see the folds of the boy's jersey on her hips, her thin eyebrows like the wings of a bird in the distance, the egg-brown skin of her thighs as she kneeled.

'So what happened,' said Rankin.

'Nothing much. She talked about the problems with her work. She's a poet.'

'Poetry in motion more like!' Rankin snorted impatiently. 'What else?'

Rankin was trying to spoil it, with his innuendo an intrusion into Hugh's awareness. Hugh wouldn't talk about it. He wanted to seal it up like a ship in a bottle, safe from the clumsy exploration of Rankin and all the others. 'So nothing happened,' said Rankin. He seemed both satisfied and disappointed. Rankin was not capable of subtlety. He could apply only one assessment. Like a collector dissatisfied unless the butterfly is pierced beneath the glass, and giving no significance to having merely seen its colours and its grace. Even at seventeen Hugh knew better than to attempt an explanation, or give any sign of being moved.

'I think she's getting pretty drunk,' he said carelessly. 'We shot a dog. It was brindled.'

'What?'

'It doesn't matter.'

'I'm told Mrs Jewell was better looking even than her daughter,' said Rankin. 'She was a beautiful woman in her day, they say.' Hugh tried to imagine Mrs Jewell as a young woman, but he could picture only Helen, and there seemed no process of evolution that could lead from one to the other. Mrs Jewell's tart intelligence and angularity of body seemed distinct from any gender.

'I have to get going,' said Hugh. 'I've got the rep cricket trials this afternoon.'

'Good on you.' Rankin wasn't able to give it any real enthusiasm however. Hugh went back to the drive, and rode down the soil and gravel track to the stone pillars of the road gate.

He promised himself he wouldn't talk about the morning with anyone, but keep it all inside. Helen would marry one of those on her mother's list, or on her own list made up in time. He expected nothing else. But he had been there at her giving up party. He understood how much was coincidence, and he didn't take any credit himself: anymore than he did when he caught the gorse in bloom on the hills he climbed behind the town, or for the one or two days in summer when there was a full flight of thistle down across the sky. Yet as Hugh rode home, leaning forward and with his arms folded across the handle-bars, he was happy enough. Sometimes coincidence itself can be a kind of blessing, and he knew as Rankin never would that receptiveness can be a virtue too.

THE BIG TIME

I guess that I became a representative player because I didn't have the sense to get out of Norman Kernahern's way. It was in the trials and I was in the Possibles against the Probables who had jerseys all the same colour and so we reckoned they were first picks. Norman was a sort of local Goliath who was in the special class at Rennick and like most in that class he was a bit older, and different. He had very hairy legs and few words. When he was given the ball and the line pointed out to him, he used to put his head down and go for it like a jersey bull. None of us in the other school teams liked to play against him because he seemed to have a strange disregard for pain — his own, or any that he might inflict.

I was what was called a breakaway, which meant that like a lot of other kids I was somewhat betwixt and between as far as speed and size went. Anyway, to be picked for both trial games was really something for me, although I didn't let on. My father was pleased when I told him. Good on you. Good on you, he said. You can make the big time if you get stuck in. Who knows. I imagined what it would be like to come home and tell him that I had been selected for the under fourteens as my brother had.

So twice I did the foolish thing and tackled Normie from the front. The usual thing was to let him go bullocking past and then try to drag him down by weight of numbers from behind. The first time I went low all right and he went down with a wallop; the second time I got one of his great, mud-caked knees fair in the face, but at least the impact jarred the ball loose from his arms and he wasn't able to run on to score. The blood ran steadily from my nose and vividly polka-dotted the winter mud; my front teeth squelched a little in their gums when I tried them between my fingers. But I heard Mr Ellenor saying to the other selector that they certainly needed tacklers, and that my brother had been a bloody good age group player. So I pretended that I wanted to get back on to see out the last fifteen minutes or so, which was certainly a lie.

That's how I made the rep team for the first and last time, even though I was in the Possibles and only three from there were picked to go to Nelson for the South Island Age Group Tournament. Four days after the last trials game the team was announced in the paper. The heading on page three was Schoolboy Tournament Sides, and after the paper had been put out onto the wood heap in the lean-to a few days later, I retrieved it, cut out the piece and kept it in a cigar box with a sliding lid that I'd found in the drum at the back of the club hotel. The wood of it was dark pink with open pores and a magical smell of vaporub and rich tobacco. Other things I kept in it were one of my father's service medals, a shilling that had been run over by a train, a photo of my standard three class with me beside Susan Wedderburn, my athletics certificate, a miniature union jack that I waved at the Queen, and the only letter that Susan Wedderburn ever wrote back to me.

How casual I pretended to be when my family saw it in the paper. My father laughed out loud, which was a rare thing for him, and said that it might be the start of something big. My brother remembered the tournament as being a whale of a time and mum said I deserved some new rugby shorts. A relative I didn't know very well, a cousin I think, rang up to congratulate me. The headmaster read our names out in assembly; mine and Sam Tuki's. He was the other boy from Colenso who made the team and was really good and later turned to League. Susan Wedderburn smiled at me with a promise in it beyond my comprehension.

My father wasn't quite as pleased when I came back with the costs set out on a banda sheet by Mr Ellenor. Hitting the big time was one thing, paying for it was another. We were being billeted in Nelson, but there was still the travel and so on. My father reckoned that the Rugby Association should be doing a great deal more in regard to assisting junior teams. Sport's all very well he said. We had several practices in the weeks before the August tournament. Mr Ellenor and Mr Hood were great on planned moves which they numbered and would shout from the sideline. Number seven, for example, I remember because I was supposed to detach early, get the ball from the half-back, run through close to the scrum and pass on the inside to Normie who would then go crashing on. I had dreams in which I executed number seven perfectly and then stood back to watch Norman Kernahern trampling down the opposition on his way to the try line.

Looking back it seems to me likely that Mr Ellenor and Mr Hood saw the tournament as the start of coaching careers of distinction. They persuaded all of us that we shouldn't leave town in the first week of the school holidays so that we were available for practices and work-outs before going to Nelson.

A Tuesday it was when we left for the tournament. We had to be at the Old Boys' Club Rooms at nine, and the frost was still on the ground. Mr Ellenor read out the billeting list before we boarded the two mini-buses that he and Mr Hood would drive. I was to stay with a Mr and Mrs James and so was Normie. I'd asked if I could go to the same place as Sam Tuki, but Mr Ellenor said that Normie wasn't up to being billeted by himself and needed a friend to look after him. Apart from having some close physical contact with Normie in the trials I didn't quite see how I fitted the bill, but you don't argue with the coach.

On the way over we had a break at Pelorous Bridge and a short jog just to free the muscles after all that sitting. Despite his strength, Normie didn't seem to have extra good wind and he puffed a lot as we ran. I was in the same mini-bus, unfortunately, because later, in the hills before Nelson, Normie was sick on the floor and the smell of it just about set the rest of us off. Mr Ellenor said that Normie had got over excited. Don't let him get over excited he said to me. I could see that the responsibility of being co-billetee was being extended considerably. How it had all come about in Mr Ellenor's mind I couldn't tell. Was it because of play number seven which figured both Normie and myself, was it because Normie had injured me in the trials and we had to be reconciled, was it just some random coincidence that we were both to stay with the Jameses. Mr Ellenor told me to make sure that Normie didn't get over excited there and be sick again in the Jameses' house. He said that Mr James was a lawyer, or an accountant, and on the Junior Advisory Committee. As he told me we were passing the mud-flats just before Nelson and despite having opened what windows we could, the smell of sick was greater than our concentration on ignoring it. Normie had his face hidden in his arms for shame and his black, pig-bristle hair gleamed in the spring sunshine.

All the teams met at a big school not far from the Cathedral. Mr Ellenor said that it was the tournament headquarters and we had a drink of raspberry cordial and some very plain biscuits while more and more teams arrived. There were some pretty big guys. It seemed to me that the Christchurch team in particular were big guys, some almost as big as Normie. And they had a great, woolly mascot which they paraded around as if they owned the place, while we had no mascot and blamed our coaches for lack of foresight. There was this opening ceremony and then a lot of talk about the various grounds and the draw before the people taking billets started to arrive and Mr Ellenor rounded us up and took us and his list to Room 15 on the ground floor where we were to meet the people to stay with. Hosts, Mr Ellenor kept calling them and it conjured up in my mind the idea of huge crowds of people, like the Midianites you get told about at Sunday School.

Anyway, Mr James wasn't there; it was his wife who came to pick us up. She had this very pale, shiny hair and pearls around her neck. On the way to her house she took us past some of the places she said were features of Nelson, but I can't remember any except the Cathedral. What does your father do, Hugh? she asked me, and then, and what does your father do, Norman?

I been sick in the van, said Normie. Mrs James had already wound down the window.

Normie and I were put in this beaut room which was extra big and had a polished, wooden floor. There were several sheep skin rugs and when Mrs James left us to unpack Normie found that if you turned the rugs over they made amazing sledges on the polished floor. Normie was really sharp at things like that. He tore down the passage with the sheepskin held in front of him and then dived on to the bedroom floor and slid the entire length before crashing into the wardrobe at the end.

I had a few goes myself, but the enjoyment was spoilt by the thought that the excitement might make Normie sick again and that anyway Mrs James wouldn't like it.

Normie had all his gear in one small, cardboard case and his boots were in a shopping bag. Despite being bigger than me, he seemed quite happy for decisions to be made for him. He'd got used to being told what to do I suppose. I did let him choose which bed he wanted and he said the one furtherest from the door because the bogey wouldn't get him in the dark. I was getting a new impression of Norman Kernahern, instead of the sort of human rock that we all feared in the footy games. His toughness was all gristle and bone, rather than something of the spirit.

He was careering that bulk of gristle and bone into the wardrobe for the umpteenth time when Mrs James came up the stairs. She took it very well, especially as she had no children herself, but she collected the sheep skins and carried them away because she said they needed cleaning.

The baas have gone, said Normie sadly.

The radio's on downstairs, said Mrs James, and I've borrowed a giant jig-saw which has all the Disney characters.

Hip-bloody-ray, I said quietly to Normie as we went down.

Mr James came home at tea time. He didn't say if he was a lawyer, or an accountant, but he was a very small man; no taller than Normie and nothing like as heavy. He had a lot of long, grey hair combed straight back from his face like a musician and he told Normie and me about each team entered in the tournament and all the planning which had gone into it. Insurance against rainy days had been his idea he said. Probably it was because he was small that we didn't have much for tea, or maybe because he had to go to a meeting almost straight afterwards. A sort of frothy omelette it was, that disappeared when you bit down on it and then slices of fruit and raw vegetables. Most of Normie's omelette seemed to gather round his mouth and I could tell he didn't think much of raw vegetables slivers for his main meal. He kept looking hopefully about for other stuff which never came, but thank god he didn't actually ask. Normie was almost as well known for his huge appetite and his huge farting as for his bullocking runs on the paddock, but Mrs James couldn't be expected to have heard of his reputation in Nelson. So he just sat there and starved. I could have done with a plate of bangers and mash myself. Mr James knew the whole draw by heart I reckon. As he had a cup of tea he told us that the next morning we played Southland and in the afternoon Mid-Canterbury. The pool games were round robin, he said. He wished us good luck before he went to his meeting and ran his fingers straight back through his musician's hair.

My mother had told me that after every meal I was to offer to help with the dishes and so I volunteered to Mrs James. I could see that it wouldn't be a long job. Why thank you, Hugh, she said, and looked at Normie who was gagging on half a carrot and said not a thing.

A few times afterwards Normie slid on his stomach across the bare bedroom boards, but it didn't work as well without the sheep skins and for most of the evening he and I were downstairs listening to the radio and pushing jig-saw pieces around. Normie quite liked the music, but was bored with just talking. Every time that Mrs James came into the room he looked up cheerfully from Pluto, or Donald, in expectation of food, but there never was any, though he took up the offer of cocoa and had three mugs of it. Normie could make spittle bubbles. Not many kids can do that. I've never been able to do it myself, but Normie could even get them to float away from his face. In all my life I've never seen anyone else do that. I wondered if it was a fluke that night because of all the cocoa that Normie had on an almost empty stomach.

A little after ten-thirty Normie and I went up to the bedroom. For a while he was happy looking out of the window at the lights of Nelson, for the house was on the hillside. Thousands of white, shimmering lights like fireflies, and other lights in special patterns like the orange ones that marked out the main thoroughfares, or the neons of the inner city. But when I came back from the bathroom he was crying. I'm so hungry, he said. That lady forgot our tea. I suppose it was worse for Normie because his stomach was empty from being sick in the minibus and he had such a thick body to maintain. You don't grow knees big enough to fill an opponent's face on omelette and vegetable slivers. Hungry, he said. I could hear his stomach rumbling and piping at its denial.

I heard Mr James come in well after eleven, and so did Normie, because his stomach stopped its noise in anticipation of food. I could have told Normie that the chances of our host bringing in a mid-night feast were not great. Normie began rocking in his bed; in a sitting position and he said Ah-ah-ah-ah-ah-ah to himself in a sing-song voice to provide some comfort in starvation. I could hear his tears in the dark.

I realized that Normie was building up to an outburst: becoming beside himself as the saying is and I remembered Mr Ellenor telling me not to allow Normie to get over excited. Hey, don't worry, Normie, I said. We'll make a raid on the kitchen. I tried to make it sound a fun thing, but I was filled with misgivings myself. If I'd been older I suppose I would have just gone along and knocked on the Jameses' door and said that Normie was especially hungry and could he please have more to eat. At the time though it didn't seem an option.

By promising Normie some food I had taken on an obligation and he came and stood by my bed; humble, expectant, large, the tears glittering in the light from the hall and his breath still uneven from his sobbing. You wait here, I said.

I crept down the passage and across the landing at the top of the hanging staircase by the master bedroom. I suppose things creak during the day just as they do at night, but you never seem to notice then. As I went down the curving stairs I tried to put a good deal of weight on the bannisters with my right hand so that the stairs wouldn't be heard. In the kitchen I felt better and once the door was closed I could turn on the light. I found a piece of cold tongue in the fridge and in the breadbin were two fresh scones. With the meat in one hand and the scones in the other I found that I couldn't lean on the bannisters going back up the stairs and I had to take even more time, having a foot lifted in the dark and my breath caught for what seemed like minutes at a time. On the landing, just outside the door which separated me from the Jameses, I had a most positive and hideous fear that I would be discovered; stolen tongue in one hand, stolen scones in the other, but I got by without it happening. Maybe Mr James was calculating wet weather insurance premiums in his sleep.

Normie thought that I had brought him life itself. He cheered up enormously as he made scone and tongue sandwiches, and as I wiped the jelly from my hands with the bed clothes I could see him outlined at the window watching the lighted city and hear him eating noisily. It would fuel him for some devastating runs against Southland in the morning I thought.

Normie however was still hungry, but I'd had enough of the business. I told him that I wasn't going down again and when he said that he'd go himself I said like hell he was; that the Jameses' bedroom door was right on the landing and that I'd had to swing down on the outside of the staircase.

Outside outside? said Normie.

Bloody right, I said. Tarzan stuff, so let's get some sleep.

Normie settled into his bed and didn't rock any more. I relaxed and after a while started to have a dream in which I won the cup for the most tries scored at the tournament and Susan Wedderburn kissed me because of it.

Normie's yelling woke me up, and the shouts of Mr and Mrs James. I ran out and from the landing could see Normie lying on the floor below and the Jameses trying to comfort him. There wasn't much any of us could do and when the doctor came he said that Norman had broken his leg in two places. He must have climbed over the bannisters for god's sake, said Mr James.

For all of the tournament I could tell that Mr Ellenor blamed me for letting Normie get over excited, even though he never actually said it. In his eyes I was a washout and I must say that I didn't have a good tournament. But then the whole team apart from Sam Tuki was poor and whether we would have won anything with Normie I don't know, but certainly I never was able to feature in number seven when I was going to go between half-back and first five and then unload to Normie as he came steaming up. Too much can be expected of you in a team I reckon. I didn't tackle anything like as well and from then on I lost a good deal of interest in the game. I left the big time for Sam Tuki.

FATHER AND SON

He watched his father eating toast; impatient at the deliberate way his father spread the butter and marmalade into each corner before he would eat. 'If we hurry,' he said, 'we could do some before we have to leave.' He meant if his father hurried, for the boy himself had finished, and sat watching. The boy's head was round, and the skin of his face clear and brown. He had combed his hair forward with his fingers, and it lay over his forehead like the worn ends of a thick rope.

'He gives me no rest,' his father said.

'You do too much for him,' said his mother. 'You give in to him.' She meant nothing by saying that. At least she didn't mean what she said. The warmth between the boy and his father was an aura. Even though she was at a distance from it, the complacency affected her. 'You two. I don't know,' she said. 'The two of you and that track.'

'He never gets tired of it. He gives me no rest does he.'

'Next year for high school he'll have to spend more time on his work.'

'We could do some though, before we have to leave,' said the boy.

The end of the shed was given over to the slot-car track. A bulb on an extension cord hung from a nail in the rafters, so that at night they could work on it if they wished. There was a tunnel and a viaduct, town streets and freeway. The boy and his father didn't need a light in summer, even before eight o'clock. They talked about the rock face to go above the tunnel. 'When it's finished,' said his father, 'we could colour some kapok fluff and glue it on as vegetation.'

'I don't want any grass and stuff on it. Just all rock towering up;

all rock glistening and high above the tunnel. Please dad.'

His father sat on the stool, pushing lacing wire through the pieces of old carton. The wire would hold the plaster of Paris for the cliff face. The boy was mixing it with practised ease. 'I could get some acrylic paint in the yard I suppose,' his father said. 'Black and grey. It looks best with multiple coats. I remember noticing something at that Pixie Town in Nelson. On one part which was supposed to be volcanic rock it looked like they'd dripped candle wax.'

'Hey, yea.'

'It's an idea isn't it.'

'Hey, yea. Candle grease.' He could see it in his mind's eye. The dark cliff above the tunnel, massy and glistening. 'Yea,' he said, drawing it out.

'Perhaps I will then.' His father's voice was off-hand, but his hands on the carton and wire were loving.

The boy's mother came out to make them leave. 'You'll both be late again. How many times do I say it.' She held the lunch bag for her husband, and soccer boots and school-bag for her son.

'He gets me carried away with this jolly set-up here.' He gripped his son by the hair, and rocked his head. 'You're right. I'll be late for work again.' The idea of his work seemed to sap his naturalness, and it was replaced by a jaunty manner which was false. He was an older father than most. As he got onto his moped his thin ankles showed between shoes and trousers, and he clenched the handle-bars as if the traffic and the day ahead posed a significant threat. His son ran off at a tangent; a steady run with his bag and boots over his shoulder. The boy was not conscious of any effort, and as he ran he considered other things.

At lunchtime the boy thought he might run down to the council bus yards to see his father, but the teacher wanted the soccer game played against the other standard six. 'Flowerday,' he said. 'You'll be captain.' The boy was accustomed to achievement. He sat in the sun to put on his soccer boots, and he thought how to beat the other standard six.

When that had been accomplished he began to think of his slot-cars again, and the modelled cliff that he and his father would build. While the teacher explained the new maths in the afternoon, the boy wondered if they should have an over-hang on the cliff face. He imagined it casting a shadow on the track and tunnel entrance from the light on the rafters. He imagined the candle wax and the glistening paint.

After school he went to see his father; jogging over the reclamation short cut, and across the railway sidings. If anyone watched him they thought him a healthy, somewhat stolid boy, but there was a secondary inwardness behind his eyes. The bus fleet was kept behind the transport depot, away from the bustle of the front offices and workshops. The yard was asphalted, and surrounded by a high fence of webbed netting. Most of the buses were still on the runs, and only the dark oil stains on the asphalt which never evaporated, showed their parks. His father's shed was in the far corner. It was filled with cleaning gear for the buses, and racks of destination plates. Some of the plates were for runs discontinued years ago his father said, but they were kept in the hut still because that had always been their place. The boy reached up as high as he could and gripped the netting. His arms took some of his weight, and there was enough slack in the netting for him to be able to sway a bit back and forth, the netting rattling softly. He could feel the warm sun on his back, and its indirect warmth through the thick, galvanised wire. He hung quite happily, and pushed himself idly back and forth with the netting as he watched the shed to see if his father was there.

Two men in suits came from the offices towards the yard. They came from the bustle of getting things done, towards the stillness of the parking yard. They stepped through the gate not far from where the boy hung on the side netting in the weeds of the railway ground. They walked briskly to show that they had urgent responsibilities. One had a moustache; and he wasn't as important as the other. The boy could tell that, because when he spoke he kept glancing at the clean-shaven man, but the clean-shaven man remained looking ahead when he said something. The clean-shaven man had an expression as though from a considerable height. A look which said isn't that so though, isn't that just so. Neither man took any notice of the boy; he may as well have been a shrub on railway property to them. With the candour of childhood he swung gently on the netting and watched them carefully.

'He'll be hiding in his shed, Mr McPhail,' said the man with the moustache. 'He spends half his bloody life hiding in the shed. Whether he spends his time playing with himself or not I don't know.' He looked quickly at his superior's face to see how his words were received. Mr McPhail gave a burst of perfunctory laughter, and kept looking ahead. He surveyed the quiet, almost empty yard. He couldn't imagine what a man could do there year after year.

'What does he actually do?' he asked.

'He's supposed to valet the buses and that. He's responsible for making sure they're all secure before the yard is locked at night.'

'We need to make economies if we can, George. Even at his level. This work could be done by a good lad in four hours a day. Give him a call, George,' said Mr McPhail.

'Oiy, Norm,' shouted George. 'Norm — an.' The shed door opened and the boy's father came out and stood.

'What's his name?' said Mr McPhail.

'Flowerday.'

'Is that right though. Jesus.'

'Yes, Flowerday. What a mouthful isn't it.'

'He's not a pansy is he?' said Mr McPhail. George laughed with Mr McPhail, pleased at the humour he had been able to provide with the name of the boy and his father.

Flowerday was walking rather stiffly towards them across the asphalt of the large parking area. George motioned again, using his whole arm as if throwing something over his shoulder. 'Shift yourself for Christ's sake Norm,' he shouted. Flowerday began to run awkwardly: more a skipping action. At a distance he put on a placating smile in anticipation, so that he appeared to grimace as he skipped. The three men gathered not far from the boy, but only his father took notice of him, and gave a fluttering gesture with one hand low by his hip. Asking forgiveness because he couldn't recognize him, intending reassurance that they'd be together soon, expressing embarrassment that he should be seen in subservience.

'Norm, this is Mr McPhail,' said George.

'I intend to be businesslike,' said Mr McPhail. 'Mr Flowerday, my presence is required to witness a formal warning issued to you by Mr Lamont that your work has not been satisfactory in various instances.' The boy watched his father's posture, heard the formal notification of all the deficiencies in execution of his father's duties, but when George and Mr McPhail turned to walk back to the offices the boy had gone. He ran purposefully through the railway sidings and over the reclamation track. His brown face was as stolid as ever, and no-one was close enough to see his eyes.

The boy's father arrived home after five. He switched off his moped, and sat by the shed. His legs were angled as props to keep the bike balanced; his thin ankles were barely a connection between shoes and trousers. His glossy, full-face helmet was twice the size of the bike's engine, and therefore ridiculous. The boy didn't come out. The father put his moped away in the shed, and saw that the new pieces for the cliff above the tunnel had been broken. 'He said the soccer ball bounced on it accidentally.' His wife came in behind him. 'He said he was sorry about it. He's gone off to play soccer now.' The boy's father stood with one of the carton pieces in his hand: the fresh plaster like whipped cream. 'It does him good, playing with kids his own age,' said his wife cheerfully. Flowerday turned the piece over and over in his hands, as if examining it; almost as if he were still interested in it. 'You'll be able to have a bit of peace and quiet before tea for a change,' his wife said.

SUPPER WALTZ WILSON

Supper Waltz loved oysters, and in the season he had them for his tea whenever his mother was on the afternoon shift. About half-past four, after we'd been playing along the cliffs or wandering in town, he'd buy his oysters. He couldn't wait any longer. If the rest of us had any money we'd buy some too, and walk up to the shelters overlooking the bay. Winter is the time for oysters, and from the shelters we would watch the leaden waters of the harbour, and the heat from the oysters and chips would make our noses run. Pongo, Graeme, Supper Waltz, and I. Supper Waltz didn't just eat his oysters; he ravished them. First he would tear off the batter, then hold the steaming oyster by its frill and bite cruelly into its centre with his sharp teeth. Sometimes as a conscious indulgence he'd eat two at once, growling with pleasure deep in his throat. It was another occasion on which we realised that Supper Waltz had a heightened perception of the world.

Children take their own situation as the universal one when they're young. My father dominated our family as naturally as a pyramid does the sands; that's why I always found the Wilson household disconcerting I suppose. Mr Wilson was a master butcher, but years ago he'd had a revelation from the Lord telling him not to work any more, and his religious conviction never wavered afterwards. He always seemed to be in his room. Scores of times I was at the Wilsons', and if Mr Wilson was mentioned he was almost always in his room. If he wasn't then he was in the lavatory singing hymns; he knew all the words, and never had to go dum-de-dah or somesuch in places. He didn't seem to have much of an ear though, and it wasn't good to listen to. Once he was singing, and Supper Waltz's eldest brother was in the kitchen.

'Arse arias again today, mum,' he said, and Mrs Wilson threw down the carrot she was scraping into the sink, and began to laugh. The carrot splashed up water on to her face, and the drops ran like tears as she laughed. Supper Waltz laughed a lot too, and I joined in the way you do when you're not sure why.

Mrs Wilson worked in the woollen mills. She often seemed to be just coming or just going.

A very matter-of-fact woman, Mrs Wilson. Tall and strong; lacking any graces. When she cycled up the rise to the house she didn't get off and wheel the bike the way other women did, but stood up on the pedals, using her weight and strength like a man, pushing right up to the gate. Pongo's and Graeme's mothers usually said hullo to me, or asked about my parents, but I don't remember Mrs Wilson saying anything at all to me — except the once. A hard woman if she wanted to be I guess, Mrs Wilson. Wherever Supper Waltz got his looks it wasn't from his mother. They had the same eyes though. The same restless, flickering eyes, like light through the wings of a bird in a cage.

Most grown-ups didn't like Supper Waltz. They were used to youngsters who were socially clumsy, and submissive to authority. The Rev. Mr Weir called him a smart aleck and barred him from the Boys' Brigade, and old Raymond detested him. Adults didn't understand the fierce vision of Supper Waltz's world, and they resented his unspoken contempt of their ways. The square of the hypotenuse, the 1832 Reform Act, were as dead leaves to Supper Waltz, and only art interested him. Old Raymond loved to ridicule him. 'And how many, Wilson, did you say you got for the test? Speak up lad. You got nothing! Well perhaps that explains why I couldn't hear anything, Wilson. I didn't hear any mark because you didn't get any mark. Not a one lad.' Raymond, with his broken teeth and first class honours degree, had to get his own back. I understand it better now. Raymond hated Supper Waltz because he neither needed nor desired anything that Raymond had; and they both knew it.

Girls knew that Supper Waltz was different too. Supper Waltz seemed old in the ways of the world. As fifth formers it wasn't easy for most of us to be the ladies' man. Pongo had a face as round and as innocent as a child's. Baby Brother, the girls called him. Supper Waltz never missed out at a teenage dance; Supper Waltz was a parochial legend of our youth. He went home with sixth form girls, and some even that had left school. Girls came looking for Supper

Waltz, some without knowing why and blushing because of it. Some girls hated Supper Waltz, they said — afterwards. Supper Waltz rarely danced in the early part of the evening. He'd hang around the door, smoking, talking, watching who went in and who went out. We'd nudge one another and snigger when the supper waltz was announced. I don't think I ever saw Supper Waltz refused by a girl.

Supper Waltz had an understanding of women all right. Like the time I wanted to go out with Fiona Hume. She was at the private girls' school. She wore a short, green skirt in the hockey games, and the inside of her thighs was flat and smooth. It used to give me a headache just watching her. Supper Waltz and I waited for her as she went to church, and I asked her to see me the next weekend. I thought she was going to say yes, but she went off laughing with the others finally without giving me an answer. She had a rather longer dress on that day, but I still got a headache. Supper Waltz didn't joke about her or anything. We went into the golf course nearby, and hunted for balls to sell. After a while I asked him why Fiona Hume hadn't said she'd go out with me. Supper Waltz had no trouble with the answer. 'It's the fairisle jersey,' he said. 'No girl will make a date with you in a fairisle jersey.' My mother had given me the jersey for my last birthday. I thought of it as part of my best clothes. 'It's a kid's jersey, Hughie, see?' said Supper Waltz frankly. 'Girls think a lot about that sort of thing.' Supper Waltz was right of course. With some of my money from potato picking I bought a denim top, and I did my hair without a part before I asked Fiona Hume again. I never told Supper Waltz about her thighs and my headaches, but the day she agreed to go out with me Supper Waltz watched her walk away and said, 'She has really good legs you know, really good legs,' and he seemed pleased for me in a brotherly way.

It might seem that Supper Waltz was always the leader, and that I was just tagging along all the time, but it wasn't really like that. There were ways in which Supper Waltz depended on me. With adults for example Supper Waltz let me do most of the talking. Even old Raymond said on my report that I was a straightforward, sensible boy. He meant predictable I think. I was in the cricket team by the fifth form, and bigger than most of the others. I kicked Wilderborne in the back when he picked on Supper Waltz in the baths enclosure. Both Pongo and Graeme were better than Supper

Waltz at some things too; Graeme was dux in the end. We all lacked the vision of Supper Waltz though; the world was sharper, brighter for him and the meaning always clear. Once Supper Waltz, Graeme and I went camping in the Rangitata gorge, and came down the rapids on lilos. The water was a good deal rougher than we thought. Graeme got thrown off his lilo and smashed his teeth out on the rocks. I went on only because I couldn't stop. I felt sure I was going to drown. Supper Waltz loved it; each time he bobbed up from the spray and turmoil of the water, he laughed and stared about as if born anew. He wanted to go down again, but Graeme and I wouldn't. That night, lying in the pup tent amongst the lupins, Supper Waltz told us that each time he'd come up from beneath the water the world seemed a different colour. Crimson the last time; after the longest spell under when his lilo capsized, everything was crimson he said. Graeme and I said nothing. The revelation rather embarrassed us, and besides, Graeme's mouth was too sore for him to speak.

Another time a group of us went into the reserve to do some geography field work with Scotty, and at the edge of one of the gullies was a cast sheep. It lay on its side at the verge of some blackberry bushes, and the flat circle of its rotation was stained with urine and droppings. The sheep's black rubber lip twitched, and its eyes bulged with mild perplexity at its own fate. Some of the class tried to stand it up, but each time it just swayed there a moment before falling stiffly on the same side, flattened like the underneath of a scone. Scotty told everybody to leave it alone, but even as we worked our way through the blackberry into the gully we could hear the sheep's hoarse, strained breathing. Wilderborne said he was going to come back after school and give it the works.

Once out of the sight and sound of it most of us could forget the sheep, but it persisted in Supper Waltz's mind. He was very quiet, and when the others were looking at some shell fossils in the limestone, I saw him crying. That would have surprised old Raymond and Mr Weir; anyone who thought Supper Waltz was so tough. He had a lot of emotion in him did Supper Waltz. He could stand up to old Raymond and the Head without a change of expression, but train whistles and morepork calls in the dark would haunt him for hours.

When I think of what happened to his father, and about Supper Waltz going away, I think of the evening I heard Mr Wilson talking about his voices. That was months before, but I always imagined him going mad right after I saw him in the kitchen. Recollection is apt to sandwich such things up, and there's a type of logic in it I suppose. I'd climbed through Supper Waltz's window, and was sitting on his bed reading until he finished his tea. Then I heard Mr Wilson talking, and I went along the passage and stood there, looking in on the angle to the lighted kitchen. I very rarely saw Mr Wilson, and with me in the dark and him in the light I got a good chance. He was younger and softer looking than his wife. He had a pale, smooth face like a schoolteacher's or a parson's; he had youthful, fair curls, and yet his fingers were stained with nicotine, and his stomach folded softly over his belt.

'I heard the voice again today,' he said earnestly.

'Did you?' said Mrs Wilson. Her tone was the mild encouragement of a mother to her child, and she continued to iron rapidly from the cane basket on the table.

'Prepare for leadership, it said. Keep yourself ready for the test.' Mr Wilson ran his hand through his bright, metallic curls, and as they sprang back I half-expected them to jangle. He seemed to be addressing a larger audience than Supper Waltz and Mrs Wilson. Like Supper Waltz he was small, and he had the strut of a small man as he walked about the kitchen. 'I will turn a righteous sword in the guts of this poor world before I'm finished,' he said. Despite the falseness of the words he said it with conviction. 'It was the voice to the left of me. That's always the strongest voice, the one to the left of me, and it doesn't hurt, not that one. I've got a feeling my leadership is near, Melanie.' That had the strangest sound of all — Melanie, Mrs Wilson as Melanie, and although no-one could see me I smiled sheepishly.

Mrs Wilson and Supper Waltz didn't find it remarkable however. 'Good,' said Mrs Wilson. She ran over a shirt-collar quickly, her thumb anticipating the iron along its length with practised ease. Supper Waltz was eating bread and cold meat, his eyes turning upwards like a sheepdog's with satisfaction as he ate.

'Everything will be sorted out then. I'll have my proper place then. I'm ready for the work.' The thought of his great work and its immediacy seemed to lift Mr Wilson. He went abruptly through to the lavatory, and there began to sing about the land of Canaan. In his absence, as in his presence, the kitchen went on as before; Mrs Wilson ironing urgently, and Supper Waltz eating his meat sandwiches as if he would never stop.

The day months afterwards, the day after it happened, was a Wednesday and Supper Waltz wasn't at school. It was a hot day, and I thought he'd probably bunked to be in the sun. Supper Waltz often took days off, and if the teachers checked up on him he'd produce notes that he'd written himself, but signed by his father. I imagined Mr Wilson signing them in his room, or on the toilet seat, as he waited for his call. Supper Waltz never explained to me why that one duty was performed by his father, when all else had been resigned to Mrs Wilson. I suspected that his mother never knew when he hadn't been at class. She came up to the school once though, summoned after Supper Waltz and old Raymond had a confrontation in the film room. We were in one of the front rooms, and I saw her arrive, pedalling right up the sweep of the drive, and she left her bike leaning on the hydrangeas by the steps to the school office. She blew her nose in a business-like way on what looked like half an old tea-towel, and strode up the steps like a man. One or two of the boys close to the window laughed, but Supper Waltz and I didn't let on we knew who it was.

But that Wednesday, after it must have happened, I was sitting in Raymond's room when the First Assistant came in. Old Raymond always made a show of rapport with his boys when there was another master in the room. 'Pop outside with Mr Haldane, Williams,' and he patted my shoulder as I passed. When the door was closed Haldane stood in the corridor for a moment, gazing absently down at the worn lino, and then up at the paper pellets which had been chewed and flicked on to the yellow ceiling. Most boys respected Haldane, although he wore some of the worst clothes in the school, and caned with distant severity.

'Stuart Wilson,' he said, and for just a moment I didn't think of Supper Waltz. None of us called him Stuart. 'You're his best friend, I understand.' It made me feel rather good that; to be singled out by Haldane as Supper Waltz's best friend. It was a form of recognition in its way. 'You know the family quite well, you're there quite often?' I told him I was. Haldane looked at me as if he were wondering how much of me was still boy, and how much had grown up. I think he decided to be cautious. 'Stuart's father is not well, and there's been a bit of an accident at their home. Mrs Wilson wants you to go round and see if you can help. Stuart's rather upset. Have you got a bike? You needn't be back before afternoon school.' As I started off down the corridor he added, 'And Williams, use your commonsense, won't you lad. Don't tittle-tattle other people's problems all round the school, will you.' That disappointed me a bit, for after all I was Supper Waltz's best friend.

I remember that someone had twisted the dynamo bracket on my bike right into the spokes, and it broke off as I was straightening it. I felt odd biking alone in the sun down that street, always crowded before. In three blocks I passed only a mother and her push-chair. I was young enough to be amazed by the realization that other people live different lives. It was like that all the way to Supper Waltz's place, hardly a car, hardly a sound, with just a few women around Direen's store, and a little kid crying at the top of Manuka Drive because his trike had overturned in the gutter.

I must have been to the Wilsons' hundreds of times, yet I felt shy arriving there then; during school time, and having been sent for. Mrs Wilson was sitting at the kitchen table, moving the butter-dish round and round with her finger. 'Come in, Hughie,' she said. I don't think she'd ever used my name before. 'Sit down. We've had trouble here, Hughie.' She was a direct woman, Mrs Wilson. Her left hand was in plaster, and the fingertips stuck out from the end of it like pink teats. With her other hand she kept moving the butter-dish on the red formica table. 'Stuart's father's had a breakdown and has had to go to hospital.'

'Oh.' I watched the butter-dish revolve, and wondered about Mr Wilson's Canaan.

'The point is Stuart's run off. I haven't seen him since last night. Do you know where he could be?'

'No.'

'He's fond of you, Hughie. He might come to see you. He's very upset. But you're his friend.'

'Supper Waltz and I have always been friends,' I said. 'Always will be.' Mrs Wilson smiled, either at the nickname or the claim of eternity; a man's smile, which divided her lined face.

'Bit of a charmer with the girls, from what I hear,' she said.

'With everyone. I mean they all like him.' I was trying to please with that admittedly. Teachers and parsons didn't like Supper Waltz, and some girls didn't — afterwards. Supper Waltz put his tongue in their mouths when he kissed them.

'His father was a popular man. He had a gift of imagination that man; but not the character to go with it.' It wasn't as cruel a judgement as it sounded, for Mrs Wilson still had a half-smile, and she stopped moving the dish for a moment. 'He was national president of the Master Butchers' Federation when he was twenty-eight.' Mrs Wilson looked past me, and it was unusual to see her at rest. 'Then he began to listen to the morepork,' she said quietly after a time, and leant her head on her knuckles as the smile died. No-one could call Mrs Wilson a dreamer though, and she was soon practical again. She got up, and cleared her throat by spitting into the sink. 'I'm going back to work this afternoon,' she said. 'I'll have to leave a note in case Stuart comes home when I'm away. You'll let me know, Hughie, won't you, if he comes to see you? Don't let him do anything silly.' It seemed my day for being treated as an adult, and I tried not to be self-conscious. Mrs Wilson came out to see me leave, and as we talked by the wash house she busied herself by pulling at the twitch in the garden with her good hand. When I rode away the bleak whiteness of the plaster on her other hand caught the sun, and I saw also in the house next door a woman watching Mrs Wilson from behind the curtains.

I slept in the upstairs sunporch, and on the Wednesday night Supper Waltz woke me by pitching clods up at the window. I was annoyed at first, because whenever he did that I had to clean the glass and sills before Mum saw the mess in the morning. Then it came back to me about Mr Wilson and the trouble. I swung out of the window, let myself hang down by the arms at full stretch, then dropped into the garden below. It was after twelve, and Supper Waltz and I went into the garage and turned on the bench light, as we always did when he came round late. He had some oysters and chips, and we ate them in silence; Supper Waltz treating each oyster as a sacrifice of significance. He didn't say anything much for a long time. He wanted the reassurance of habit; to test some part of the old way and find it the same.

'Dad's a loony,' he said finally, turning his face from the light. 'He's a bloody loony. They took him off last night.' Even though it was Supper Waltz's dad, and I felt sorry for them both, I couldn't help being curious about the way it had been. 'Howling like a wolf or something, you mean?' said Supper Waltz when I asked him. 'Nothing like that. He was going out with no clothes on, to start his mission for Christ. He broke Mum's arm in the door when she tried to stop him. Said his time was come. His time had come all right.' Supper Waltz showed a depth of cynicism that aged him. 'You can say that again. He locked himself in the lav, Hughie, when they came; kept shouting and singing. In the lav, aye. Jesus!' Supper Waltz laughed in a harsh, pent-up way, and the tears showed in the light of the bench bulb. The paper on his knee shook with laughter, and the few chips that we had left, because of their black eyes, danced in the salt.

It seemed fitting in a way, Mr Wilson locking himself in the lavatory; it had always been a refuge for him. I didn't say that to Supper Waltz, instead I told him that his mother was waiting for him to go home. 'No,' he said, 'I'm not going home. I'll write to her in a day or two. Tell her that. Tell her I'm all right and so on, but not what I'm going to do.'

'What are you going to do?'

'I'm off up to Christchurch tonight. Danny's got a job for me in Lyttelton. As soon as I can I'll be on one of the big overseas ships. You know, European ports and all that.' Supper Waltz's brothers were all seamen, as if united in some quest. He had a brief period of bravado, and got carried away describing all the things he was going to do as a sailor, but I knew he was churned up inside. It showed in his restlessness, and the flickering eyes like light through the wings of a bird in a cage.

Before he went I crept back upstairs, and got eleven shillings for him. It was all I had, but I gave him the two flat tins of Abdullah cooltips as well; I always kept them to smoke on weekend nights when I went out. I turned out the garage light, and went with Supper Waltz down the street a bit so we wouldn't be heard outside the house. Supper Waltz kept talking urgently about all the things that lay before him; I think that once started he was more set on convincing himself than me. Although I was his best friend, and he'd come to me, I felt for the first time there in the dark street that Supper Waltz had already gone; he'd cast off from the rest of us, and was on his way. He'd made the break. The exhilaration of it seemed to separate us. 'See you, Hughie. Wish me luck, Hughie.' His fierce mood drove him running down the pavement, until he was lost in the shadows of the trees around the orphanage.

If it had been me, or Graeme, or Pongo, they would soon have caught us, but I didn't think they'd catch Supper Waltz if he didn't want them to. Supper Waltz knew the way of the world; Supper Waltz would look after himself, you bet, I told myself. Keep running, Supper Waltz, don't let the morepork get you.

HALF A CROWN

In our family nobody drank. In our Methodist household even the need for discussion of it never arose. Had it not been opposed on moral grounds, it would have been held indefensible on economic ones. My father was not a man to pour money down his throat, as he once said. He despised waste and wasters. Smoking and drinking were signs of weakness to my father, though the shape of a woman was acknowledged to be real temptation, and one that deserved discipline to resist. My grandfather came from Wales. He said that we were descended from the Prince of Powys. Little practical legacy remained, and he had been an assisted immigrant. He had an even greater horror of needless expense than my father, and was very bald when he died. Drinking tea is like drinking silver, my grandfather used to say. I was young when he died, and that's the only saying in which I can hear his voice. He was two steps closer to the Prince of Powys that I. Better times in this country had accustomed us to drinking tea without guilt, but alcohol was seen as a disfigurement: like having one leg shorter than the other, or ringworm scars.

So when I was twelve and saw a drunk man sitting outside our gate, I knew he was to be despised. He was a thin man, and rested his knuckles on the footpath as he sat in the early afternoon sun. He wore a grey suit that held its creases well, and a cream shirt of elegance. I sat with my back in the hedge, and watched him. I whistled, and juggled the small crab-apples which I had for throwing at birds. He looked at me and smiled. 'What's your name?' he said, and I told him. 'Mine's David too,' he said, without surprise at the coincidence. He smiled at some of the other things around, but didn't ask their names. He smiled knowingly at the gatepost, and the knuckles of one hand, as though these things had winked at him or nudged him to provoke his smile. 'David you must help me home,' he said. He moved his legs back and forth. His brown, polished shoes scuffed on the pavement, but the upper part of his body didn't move. He smiled, sheepishly, as if someone had played a trick on him. 'Help me up, David,' he said.

I was supposed to go sledging on the Wither Hills. I'd told the others that I would, and I had some fat wrapped up, to grease the runners. The drunk David held opportunities though, I could see that. I could sense the weakness in him revealed by the drink, and when he pumped his legs I heard money in his coat pocket. I looked back through the hedge, and up the path. I couldn't see any one of our family. By taking one arm I helped David up. He was able to walk quite well, but he was too relaxed and trusting to be sober. 'I've been to the funeral of my best friend,' he said as we walked. He took one of the crab-apples from me and examined it closely. He began to cry, holding the bridge of his nose with his fingers, then abruptly he smiled again, and tucked the crab-apple in his top pocket. The tears were still visible on his face. They were like a sudden sunshower, and then he was smiling again, and he walked on. He waved one arm grandly. 'I've been to my friend's funeral,' he said very loudly; the way people who have been drinking sometimes do. He looked about expectantly, as if people should come from their houses to ask him questions about his best friend's death.

'George,' he said. His voice was quiet again. He stumbled on the top plate of a water main, and reared back, amazed at its vindictiveness. He looked at me, and couldn't remember me. He made circles in the air with one hand as he thought. 'David,' he said. 'That's it. David. I'll be forgetting my own name next.' We both had a laugh at that. 'I'm pretty much cut up about it. George and I saw a lot of years together. I thought there would have been more than came. Take away the family, and very few bothered. A lot of people I know he helped, they never came.'

'How much further?' I said. I hadn't altogether given up the idea of biking out to join the others for sledging.

'George was fifty-nine,' he said. 'Not old, fifty-nine, is it? Do you think I look fifty-nine?' It's difficult to tell with old people, just how old they are. But he looked old all right. He had plenty of hair, but his eyelids had multiple folds, and he breathed heavily through his mouth as he walked. 'George and I were always going to buy a few acres by the bridge, and grow berry fruits for the early market. George's family had been in small fruits. It's very mild all year there.'

David's house was neat. A neatness that suggested a sense of maintenance, rather than a love of plants. There were shell casts in the centre of the concrete drive to the garage. I could tell David had a wife, because each window had a curtain tied at an angle. As I looked she came out onto the porch, and stood there with her arms folded, saying nothing. A grown woman, with her arms folded and a straight face can be a forbidding sight. She looked to me like a woman who had no time for the weakness of drink.

'Here we are, David,' he said. He leant on the wall, as if even though it was home, he knew that George couldn't accompany him inside. That once he went in, returned from the funeral, then George was just another dead and buried; best friend and all.

'Give us some money,' I said. 'I came all the way to help you home, and I've got to go now.' Things hadn't worked out as I'd hoped. The demand was more direct than I had intended, but I reckoned time was short.

'You want money?' said David with a smile. His wife was still watching us. I turned my face away a bit, in case she remembered who I was sometime.

'Give us half a crown, and I'll help remember George for you.' It was the best I could come up with on the spur of the moment. He took some coins from his pocket, and they lay in the palm of his hand. There were two half-crowns. They looked even bigger than I remembered them. I could enjoy myself for a week on half a crown. There is no coin today fit to match with half a crown.

'If I'd given you half a crown before,' he said earnestly, 'you would've come to George Langord's funeral, wouldn't you?'

'Yes,' I said, and it was so.

'There were a lot of people who knew him that I should have offered half a crown to,' he said. His wife seemed to be getting larger on the porch: not moving, but sort of looming up as if she were about to come out to us. 'Can I have it then?' I said, and as he didn't move his hand away, I took a half-crown from amongst the other coins in his hand. It was heavy, and I could feel the thick, milled edge of its circumference. David hardly seemed to notice. The alcohol had reached right into the centre of him, and on the dark side of the moon he saw the shadows of things of vast priority.

'Come to my funeral instead, David,' he said. 'I'm going to be worse off than George when the time comes I think.' His wife was walking deliberately down the steps of the porch. Her arms were still ominously folded.

'See you,' I said. David didn't answer. He sat on his roughcast wall, with one arm on the letter box. A grown man doesn't sit on his wall in the middle of the afternoon, and consider his funeral, unless the drink is to take the blame.

I walked casually away down the road, then once round the corner I sprinted a block, so that if his wife followed, she wouldn't be able to see which way I went.

CABERNET SAUVIGNON WITH MY BROTHER

I walked the last three kilometres to my brother's place. I was lucky to have hitched as close as I did. Along the flat through Darfield and Kirwee early in the morning I'd done a good deal of walking, but then a tractor repair man took me to within three kilometres. He told me he'd been working on the hydraulics of a new Case harvester which cost eighty thousand dollars.

I love the accumulated heat of the Canterbury autumn. When you rest on the ground you can feel the sustained warmth coming up into your body, and there are pools of dust like talcum powder along the roads. It's not the mock tropicality of the far north, but the real New Zealand summer. It dries the flat of your tongue if you dare to breathe through your mouth. After spending the vacation working on the Coast, I was happy to be back in Canterbury.

My brother Raf lived on seventeen hectares of gravel close to West Melton. He had been a tutor in economics at Lincoln, but resigned on a matter of principle. He said it was a form of hypocrisy to pretend any skill in financial affairs, when the best salary he could command was that of a tutor. Raf said that the most important things to achieve in life were privacy and revenue. At West Melton on seventeen hectares he had privacy, but the income was precarious. Raf's best crop was manoeuvres. He said he received a small but consistent return from manoeuvres. The army paid him for access to the river bed. Heavy manoeuvres was the better paying crop he said, but harder on the ground.

As I walked up the natural terrace to Raf's place, the heat shimmer on the river bed was already beginning. The stones in Raf's paddocks didn't seem to have become any less numerous. I noticed that because last time I visited my brother, he told me that ploughing only brought them up, and that picking them off was uneconomic. Raf believed that if the ground was grazed naturally, and just a little super added from time to time, then worm action would increase the height of the soil until the stones were eventually covered right over. He said he read a report of French research on it in Brittany. Raf had a knack of finding theoretical justification for his lifestyle.

He was working on his motor-bike when I arrived. It was an old Norton 500 cc, an enormous single pot machine, and his only form of transport. With it he towed a trailer large enough for ten bales of hay. He left the front tube hanging from the tyre, and came down the track to meet me. 'Ah, Tony,' he said, and took me by the shoulder. 'I hoped to see you before the term began.' His blue eyes seemed bleached from the sun, and his hair and eye-brows were nearly white. 'I told myself you'd come,' he said. Although he was my brother, he was about fourteen years older than me; we were like uncle and nephew in some ways. I was aware of the emphasis of undisguised pleasure in his voice. 'I've got quite a lot of beer at the moment,' he said proudly. 'I sold another dozen lambs last week.' To have revenue to share, as well as privacy, made him feel his hospitality was complete.

'I can't stay the night. Lectures start tomorrow. I should have been in today, really.'

'Well, we've the day together then,' said Raf, 'and you'll get out sometime during the term.'

I went with Raf into his house, and he put into his pigmy fridge as many bottles of beer as it would hold. The kitchen floor had a slant, and when the fridge was operating the vibration caused it to creep from the wall, inch by inch. I could see it, as we sat at the table with our coffee, shuffling up to Raf's shoulder like a prototype robot. 'It takes about seven minutes to reach the table,' said Raf. He tolerated it because it never broke down; just had to be pushed back to the wall every seven minutes. 'I have to switch it off when I go outside,' he said.

Raf felt no obligation to ask about our parents. Not that he disliked them; it was his way of showing that his friendship with me was apart from any other connection between us. He knew I'd tell him anything that he should know. 'You seem happy here still,' I said.

'Happiness is related to the level of expectation,' said Raf, and he pushed back the fridge. 'To be the mayor of Wellington, or the second richest farmer in Southland, is a gnawing futility if you can only be satisfied by being Prime Minister. Our education system should be directed to inculcating as low an expectation as possible in every child, and then most of them could grow up to be happy.' Raf's spur of the moment principle paid no heed to envy, but then he was working from the premise of his own nature. My brother was one of the minority who didn't compare themselves with others. He was self-sufficient in his ideas and ambitions. He enjoyed simple things; like being able to produce a meal for me from his property. We went outside, taking some beer with us, and I helped Raf to fix the front tube. As we did so, he laid out his plans for our lunch. 'If only we'd had rain,' he said, 'then there would have been mushrooms. I've been spreading the spores year by year. Now I get cartons full at times, and take them in to sell. Everything's right for them now, except the rain.'

'I'm not all that fussed on them anyway,' I said, just so that he wouldn't feel my expectation had been high.

'I've been saving some rabbits though. Down by the pines. And I've got plenty of eggs and vegetables. We could have chook, but fresh game is better.' Raf thought we should cull the rabbits before we had too much beer, and we went off over the stones and brown grass of his seventeen hectares towards the pines. 'You're doing accounting and economics, aren't you,' he said.

'Law. I'm doing law.'

'I found there wasn't much privacy in economics. I should say that law would be much the same; more revenue probably, but no privacy.' Raf stopped, and enjoyed the privacy of his land for a moment. The small terraces and scarps vibrated in the heat. The bird calls were out-numbered by the muted sound of firing from the West Melton butts. 'I've been thinking of going out of sheep into Angora goats,' said Raf. 'I read an article saying they're much more profitable per head; ideal for smaller properties. Three rabbits?' He tagged on about the rabbits after a pause, when we had started to walk towards the pines again. 'Is one and a half rabbits enough for you?'

'Fine.'

'I've been keeping an eye on these. There's nearly a dozen here. I've been looking forward to a special occasion so I could use some.' Raf walked in an arc behind the pines, so that we would come from the broken slope where there was gorse and briar. He shot two rabbits quickly with the twelve gauge, and then had me walk through the pines and flush another out to make the three.

Raf and I sat on the front step of his house, and he cleaned the rabbits, as I peeled the potatoes. He went over the various ways in which the rabbits could be combined with the other food we had. We ate those rabbits several times over before we had lunch. They were good at last though: with potatoes, pumpkin, cheese sauce, boiled eggs and beer. Repletion made Raf even more relaxed and thoughtful. 'You get plenty of girls at the university I suppose,' he asked me. For the first time there was a hint of dissatisfaction in his voice. 'Girls don't seem much interested in privacy. I had a woman out here before Xmas. She did a lot of screen printing. She seemed to like it here for several weeks, but then she began to mope. She said she found the landscape oppressive. She wasn't a very tall girl, but big where it mattered mind you.' My brother was at a loss to explain why anyone would prefer the city. 'I have to go into Christchurch now,' he said. There was a note of grievance. He saw it as a lack of consideration; the screen printing girl choosing to go back to town.

'Maybe it's the old house,' I said. 'Women have higher expectations there, I suppose.'

'I bought a new bed for us. A brass one; original. It cost me a fat lamb cheque. She hated anything artificial: plastic, vinyl, nylon, veneers, anything like that.' There certainly wasn't much of such material in Raf's house; almost everything looked pre-war. Even the walls were tongue and groove. 'She was a nice girl in many ways,' Raf said.

In mid-afternoon a visitor came. 'It's McLay,' Raf said. 'He's bought the big place up the road. I forgot all about him. He's come to look at my bore and pump.' McLay was a farmer of self-importance; one of these men who walk in a perfectly normal manner, but whose evident conceit makes them appear to swagger. He parked his European car at an angle which best displayed its lines, and his sense of complacency grew as he came closer to the house.

'Seen better days I'd say,' he said, and he tapped with his shoe at the decayed boards close to the ground along the front of the house. 'I like a place in permanent materials myself,' he said. 'Always have, always will.' Raf was never defensive about his property. He considered it too much of a blessing to need its weaknesses concealed.

'Most of the exterior is shot,' he said frankly. 'We had rabbit for lunch.' McLay was somewhat baffled by that, and suffered a subtle loss of initiative.

McLay would have taken his car to the pump, but Raf said it was easier if we sat in the trailer behind the Norton. McLay found it difficult to maintain his dignity there. He sat very upright, with one hand on the side to limit the bouncing, and with the other he tried to repel Raf's greasy tools, which clattered around us. Raf had one bore sunk into the gravel, and he ran off water to his troughs. When he reached the place he switched off the motor-bike, and sat there enjoying the sun. 'Never seems to run dry, this bore,' he said. 'It's with the river being so close I suppose.' McLay had scrambled from the trailer, and was wiping his wrist on the grass to clean it, after warding off Raf's grease-gun. He felt a need to disassociate himself from Raf's scale of farming.

'I'll need to put in perhaps a dozen of these bores,' he told me. 'I've 350 hectares you see, and I hope to irrigate from them as well.'

'I only need to run it for an hour or so each day,' said Raf. He lifted the rusted kerosene tin which protected the motor.

'Mine will have to be electric, with remote switches. I won't be able to spend all day mucking about with petrol engines,' countered McLay. Raf wound up the starting cord, and pulled with no result. 'Gives a bit of trouble does it,' said McLay. Raf tried again and again; the only result was one cough, which flicked the starting cord up to give Raf a stinging blow across the face. McLay gave an understanding laugh. 'Pity it's not Briggs and Stratton. They're the only small motor, I always say. I think you've flooded it.' Raf seized the choke, fully extended it, and bent it across the motor. McLay was quiet. Two veins began to swell beneath the skin of my brother's forehead. They made an inverted Y the colour of a bruise. He tried twice more with the cord, attempts of elaborate calmness, then he went to the trailer and brought back the crow-bar. He systematically beat the four-stroke motor until the various attached parts had broken away. The crow-bar made a solid crump, crump sound of impact, and the pipe from the bore rattled in its housing. Some of Raf's sheep stopped grazing to regard him for a while, then resumed feeding. McLay had an uneasy smile, and his eyes switched furtively back and forth from Raf to me.

By the time Raf had finished, the veins in his forehead had subsided, and he wiped the sweat away with a sense of achievement. 'Never underestimate the perversity of objects,' he said. 'Never let them get away with it. A switch won't function, a fitting or tool won't work, then before you know — open revolt. Don't give an inch. Did you hear what I said, McLay? Never underestimate the perversity of objects.'

'I'd better be on my way now,' said McLay. There was an increasing air of placating wariness about him, as he realized the full extent of my brother's eccentricity.

'I'm going to use a windmill here,' said Raf. 'I should really have fitted one long ago. We're going to have to get back to wind power a lot more in this country.'

McLay rode back in the trailer without attempting to speak against the noise of the Norton, and when we reached the house he went off with a minimum leave-taking. 'An odd sort of chap. Didn't you think?' Raf said. There was no irony apparent in his voice.

Raf brought out more beer, and we sat again on the front step to drink it. The rural delivery car went past his gate without stopping. 'At Lincoln,' he said, 'the postman was a woman. She used to pedal about in yellow shorts, and her legs were very strong and brown.' He paused, and then said, 'So very brown,' in a wistful way. 'She used to like me making puns about her having more mail than she could deal with. I have to go to Christchurch now.' The inconvenience of it rankled. 'I thought I might have had a letter from the Agricultural Department with information about goats,' he said. 'I intend those to be my two priorities this year: goats and the windmill.'

My brother's prevalent attitude to life was one of convinced cheerfulness, yet the non-arrival of the Department's letter concerning the goats, and the poignant recollection of the Lincoln post-girl's legs, had brought him as close to depression as I had ever seen him. The drink too, I suppose; we'd had quite a lot to drink. I felt it was a good time to tell him of my present. 'I brought you a present.'

'Thank you.'

'Cabernet Sauvignon. It's only New Zealand, but it's a medal winner, and four years old. I remembered you liked it best.'

The secret of Raf's joy in life was his appreciation of all the pleasures, irrespective of scale. He got up from the step in excitement. 'What a day!' he said. I got the bottle from my pack, and we had an uncorking ceremony. Raf put the bottle on the step to breathe and warm.

'We won't have any more beer now until after the wine,' he said. 'We don't want to be unable to appreciate it. Afterwards it doesn't matter.'

'I'll have to go at six or seven. I don't want to have to hitch into Christchurch in the dark.'

'Right. I'd take you in, but I've only got one helmet, and the lights on the bike aren't going.'

Raf seemed to have forgotten his disappointment about the goats and other things; his thin face was alive with speculative enterprise again. 'What to have with the cabernet?' he said. 'We can't drink a good wine with just anything.' The full sophistication of a mind which had achieved honours in economics, was given to the problem, and while the world grappled with the exigencies concerning inflation, corruption, guerrilla warfare, spiritual degeneration and environmental pollution, Raf and I sat amidst his seventeen quiet hectares at West Melton, and discussed the entourage for our cabernet. My brother was a great believer in immediate things.

We had peas and baked potatoes, red tinned cabbage and corn. We ate it from plates on our knees, as we sat on the front step. Raf talked to me of his experiences on the continent, and how bad the *vin ordinaire* was in the south of France. He had some good wine glasses, and we raised them to the evening sun to admire the colour of the wine. Raf invited me to forget university, and join him on his goat and windmill farm. 'Economics is a subject that destroys an appreciation of spiritual things,' said Raf.

'Law. I'm doing law.'

'Same thing,' said Raf. 'Probably worse.' He became so carried away in trying to persuade me of the deadening nature of formal studies, that he absent-mindedly kept the last of the cabernet sauvignon for himself, and so I fell back on beer. 'If you'd seen some of the places I have: Bangkok, Glasgow, Nice, then the value of privacy would be clear to you. Space brings the individual dignity, Tony. Herd animals are always the least attractive. Have you noticed that? I think that's one of the main reasons I want to move from sheep to goats. Goats have individuality, it seems to me.'

'A goat suits a name.'

'That's my point.' Raf sat relaxed on the step, his shingle land spreading away before him.

Just on twilight Raf took me down to the East Melton corner on the Norton. He drove carefully, conscious of the drink we'd had. 'Come out and see me soon,' he said. 'I meant what I said about forgetting economics, and joining me here to live.' I watched him ride off, without lights, and cautious of the power of the motorbike. I could hear it long after he was out of sight, and I imagined my brother riding up his track, over the stones, towards his disreputable house. To resist the maudlin effects of the wine and the beer, I lay down in the long grass; out of sight of the road. I rested my head on my pack, and slept for an hour or so.

So I ended up hitch-hiking into the city in the dark after all. I was lucky though, for after walking a few minutes, I was picked up by a dentist and his daughter. Her name was Susan. We talked about cars. I tried not to breathe on Susan, lest she think me a typical boozy student. The dentist said he'd been having trouble trying to get the wheels balanced on his Lancia. 'Never underestimate the perversity of objects,' I said. The dentist liked that, and so did Susan. They had an appreciation for a turn of phrase. Raf would have enjoyed its reception, for incantations are rarely effective beyond the frontiers of their own kingdom.

THE BANK SECTION

Further from the town, about half an hour's walk from the bridge, was the bank section. A rough strip of willows, gorse, broom and lupins on both sides of the river, but it seemed then like a continent. There was even an island, though on one side the channel was narrow and the water sluggish so that you could almost reach the shore by jumping. The island was a favourite place for setting whitebait nets in the season, but the soft material rotted out quickly, unlike the wire gauze that the adults used. Sometimes you saw the Maori trudging past with kerosene tins half full, or more, and showing no emotion at the enormity of their catch. You could get those small crays too, always coming from behind to grab them high on the back where they couldn't reach with their pincers. You boiled them in the billy under the willows and then scooped out the white flakes from beneath their tails to eat.

'Let's build a tree hut in the macrocarpas by the tip road and we can look out and see if anything decent gets dumped.'

'Let's make huts in the old cars.'

'Na, it stinks there. Phew, a bloody stink.'

'Sure does. What a bloody stink and the gulls shitting all over, but there's rats there all right. Wally and a few of us went after them a few days ago.'

'I was there too.'

'Yea, well then you remember the size of some of them. Bloody wopcackers.'

'Let's get into them.'

'Na. It's useless without a dog. Wally's got a foxy, see. That's what you need, otherwise it's useless.'

'We could go round to Wally's and pick him up. There's oodles of time.'

'Wally's mum went crook because of the stink all over the dog last time. She won't let him take it to the dump any more. Besides, Wally's pretty much a pill except for his dog.'

'Dirty minded. Always on about the size of his dawk and how he's going to root Camille Browne.'

'Fat chance there.'

'No, we don't want him without the foxy, the pill. He's all mouth.'

'He has got a fair dawk though, hasn't he.'

In the shingle pools you could catch bullies to sell to the trout fishermen for half a crown a dozen if they were a decent size. You had to use a hook with no barb so that their mouths didn't get torn. They would lie together in the carrying jar and mouth rhythmically in despair. There were plenty of eels as well, best caught at night with lines and flares when rotten eggs and stink meat had been placed to attract them. You never ate them; they weren't silver bellies anyway. Eeling was more a ritual of courage against the stories of taniwha in the dark and no matter how big the one you caught, there was always the story of the one so much bigger; as each billy goat gruff had a larger brother.

'What about bird-nesting?'

'Far too late now, you commel. Most of them have hatched and you couldn't blow any that were left anyway.'

'Peter reckons Mr Prentice at the Camping Ground pays six-pence for thrushes' and pukekos'. He made a mint last year.'

'Yea, and he'll be bloody pleased with you for spreading the word.'

'Prentice'll pay two shillings for a hawk's egg. They're all blue with just black squiggles that Chows can read their fortunes in because all hawks came from China at first.'

'Bullshit, Normie.'

'What'll he pay for sparrows'?'

'Nothing for sparrows' of course.'

'Bullshit about hawks' eggs with writing on them, Normie. You're so easily sucked in.'

'You seen one then?'

'You don't have to see one.'

'There you go. You've never seen one.'

'Two shillings is a fair bit for an egg. Maybe we could find some.'

'Well, you won't find any round here. Hawks' nests will be in cliffs and that won't they.'

'Why should they?'

'Yea, why?'

'You're stuck on that one aren't you.'

'A bird that flies high, nests high. Stands to reason doesn't it, see. What do you all know. Fly high, nest high. That's the way it is. A sparrow now nests low, doesn't it, and a blackbird up a bit, and you've got to climb pretty high for a magpie don't you.'

'Yea, that's true.'

'Skylark nests on the ground though.'

'Yea, but that's different isn't it.'

'How?'

'Oh, shut your gob.'

Each of the swimming holes had its own advantages and dangers, like the rope that you could swing out on over the long pool, and the sunken branches in the bend pool which caught and drowned Ben Nairn who had been the best runner in the school. You wore khaki shorts and no shoes in the summer so that your toes spread out and gave an almost prehensile grip for climbing, and the soles toughened so that you walked and ran through rough ground and streams and only the odd broken bottle close to the roads, or the tip, was able to cause a gush of sudden blood.

'All this mucking around. I reckon I'll go after bullies and sell them to my uncle. I'm going to get one of those Colt slug guns in the mail order.'

'My brother's got one. It's not all that hot. You've just about got to shove it up anything's bum to do any good.'

'It's not the same. Your brother's only fires bee-bees and hasn't any power hardly. The Colt Frontier model air gun fires slugs, see, with a dinkum wallop. I reckon you could bring down wild pigs with it even.'

'Bullshit.'

'Bullshit yourself. Just because you haven't got one.'

Willow will sprout from almost any part as long as there's moisture. Even those half-bulldozed, or blown down, will strike again and let down a beard of roots into the silt.

On the heavy, over-hanging branches you could lie to pick out old man trout at his station, so much larger than the ones you tickled with one hand beneath the bank.

'Russell found a new frogging pond, didn't you.'

'I said not to tell everyone.'

'I'm not. Just us here.'

'Well, don't go telling everybody. I know you jokers. You'll be over and have the place cleaned out with half a chance.'

'Where is it then?'

'I'll show you later.'

'You're bullshitting. Russell's bullshitting.'

'Where is it then.'

'I reckon I'd know any new ponds. I know this place better than anyone.'

'Yea, but the river's changed since last year, hasn't it.'

'Where is it then.'

'They're proper bull-frogs. The real dark, dark green ones and that big you need two hands to grip them.'

'Yea?'

'Yea.'

Generally there were three of you, though not *ménage à trois*. Sometimes four, or five. Any more and schism would almost certainly set in, with some getting the pip with others, gathering sufficient support to go swimming rather than frogging, or spying on lovers rather than scouting in the tip for metal to sell. Three is that comfortable number which allows democracy a decision, but still persuades the solitary minority to go along with it. During the fiercest weather you would be ambushed all day by the exploding pods of the broom, or more alarmingly by steers turned out in the river bed by the cockies for cheap grazing despite the toot. They could in their turn be tracked by their dung and prints in the sand and assailed by lupin spears and slingshot.

'It stands to reason, I suppose. I never seen as many tadpoles about as this year.'

'Russell says these big bull-frogs must have been there for years.'

'After a swim at the top hole we could go after them. The towels would do to keep them in.'

'It's no use taking heaps just for the hell of it, even if we can catch them. I get brassed off with jokers like Wally and Jonesy who just torture them all the time: put straws in their bums and blow them up and that. You need a proper place to keep them.'

'Wally's a cruel begger.'

'Maybe the girls will be at the top hole for a swim. Wendy Annis said they were coming.'

'She always says they will, but they hardly ever do. It's too far for them to walk. They don't like to sweat at all. They'll go to the town baths.'

'I don't like the way Wally picks on little jokers all the time. He needs a bloody thumping himself and I'm about ready to give it to him. He's got a nasty streak in him I reckon, and he broke the gears on my bike, but wouldn't let on.'

The wonder of it was that no matter how closely you mapped the three or four miles in your head, a winter with its floods created a new land to be explored all over again. Old channels rejuvenated, a new swimming hole, a stop bank and groin arisen from adult providence, a battered canoe beached on the island, a pair of black swans nesting in the inland place you called the lagoon.

'Tomorrow we ought to take the sledges up to the crossing. All that grass is dry and smooth now and you fairly hum down the hill. Last Sunday we all went up. What a day.'

'You didn't tell me.'

'Well, I'm telling you now. You were away or something.'

'I sand-papered the runners yesterday and then greased them up again. Polished it up like hell. She'll go like the clappers now.'

'Last time yours wasn't so hot. Kept digging in somehow.'

'Arthbutt's got a bottler. A real screamer.'

'Yea, but he didn't build it. I reckon mine is faster really, only last time he kept pushing off better, or something.'

'I pushed off as good.'

'Yea, but last time I didn't have her greased up. I got her greased up this time, you wait. Arthbutt will be eating my dust all day. And what a drongo he looks with those gloves to protect his hands. He's up himself I reckon with this new sledge.'

'Just because he won't let you have a go.'

'Won't let hardly anyone have a go. Selfish sod.'

'Is there any water up there this year? I don't want to bike all that way with the sledge if there's nowhere to swim. You get bloody hot up there and there's always a head wind on the way back. Most of the time there's a head wind going up too. I don't know what it is.'

'I bet Arthbutt's dad built his. On his own he couldn't build a tin dunney. He's useless. Remember that breadboard he made at school and where the inlay was supposed to be he had a hole right through the friggin thing!'

'Useless.'

'Yea, well I'm not going if there's no water in the hole.'

'Aw, come on, Nobby. That slope's just right at the moment and your sledge is up to Arthbutt's, I bet. Grease her up like hell and you'll be into that gorse at the bottom before you know what's happened.'

'That's another thing; that bloody gorse. I reckon we should find another course.'

Cicadas kept a chorus up all through the day. You could creep to within an inch or two, following the sound, until at last your eyes would penetrate the camouflage and you could snatch them in the sudden cup of your hands. Ants' nests, skinks like molten metal, leaving you with just a tail to tell of it. A bee swarm which Ben poked with a stick and which nearly stung him to death. It had hung like a great rotten orange. Butterflies that trembled at the water's edge, long-legged spiders that could skate on the meniscus and lavae which jacked down from the surfaces of stagnant pools which bore the slightest film of blue as if a drop of oil had been added to each one. You could lift the grey, inoffensive aged cattle turds like lids and find beneath pale, twisted grass stems which had been denied the sun. Mallards swished over in fixed wing descent towards the willowed pools and smaller spoonbills dabbled in the cress and frog-porridge. Away from the river bed the stock tracks were worn into the dry ground, just the width of a single tyre and meandering across small terraces with rabbit scrapes and through the lupins and the broom without particular direction, let alone an urgent destination. For animals travel is just a circle of nourishment after all.

'You reckon we can beat the Celtic guys on Saturday?'

'We'll do them properly.'

'Piss all over them.'

'Yea? Well that's easy for you. You're not even in the team.'

'I always come to watch though, don't I.'

'Yea, you do.'

'So I see all the play and can get a better idea of the overall game and who's playing well, can't I.'

'Maybe you can. Good on you, spud.'

Sometimes, if you were sitting very quietly in the evening, you would see a rat making an arrowhead ripple as it crossed, or a weasel flicker from one piece of cover to the next. A kingfisher occasionally sat on one of the mai-mai in the lagoon, self-effacing in demeanour despite the opulence of its feathers.

'Old Piper says there's an extra cricket practice on Wednesday to be ready for the quickie. He sends them down, by Jesus.'

'There's those dancing classes after school on Wednesday. For those who want to go to the social.'

'I can see Piper being pleased to let us off for that.'

'Who gives a toss for bloody dancing anyway.'

'That's okay until the socials and then you've got to stand around like a dummy because you can't ask anyone to dance. And you have to watch Simone Browne with Anthony Sinclair.'

'Jesus, that Simone though, aye.'

'Good enough to eat.'

'I don't know that it is, but I get a headache just looking at her.'

The lagoon was the best place for skimming. You could choose the flattened, round greywacke stones and send them bouncing upon the water with a quick, underhand throw. Nichol Carter once threw a skimmer which bounced fourteen times and there were three witnesses. Another time Nichol found a bay horse stuck in a bog hole by the big macrocarpa, but when he got help the men killed it accidentally while trying to free it. After that Ben crossed the bog hole for a bet, but some said he cheated because he lay on his stomach to do it.

'What Simone sees in that pill Sinclair I just don't know. Can't figure it out. I beat him hands down in the sports didn't I, and it made no difference at all. I just don't know.'

'It's because he's got all them sisters probably and knows how to say things.'

'And he wacks on the hair oil, doesn't he.'

'Anyway, this time I'm going to the dancing lessons and not have to stand around like a dummy all night.'

'Old Piper won't like it.'

'Yea, well stiff to him. He can put it in his piper and smoke it.'

'Ha, yea.'

'I'm just not going to be a dummy again this year. No siree.'

'He played breakaway for Wanganui, years ago, old Piper did.'

On the dry terraces were plenty of those low plants with furry, white-grey leaves that you could wipe your bum with. Tobacco plants wasn't their real name. Foxgloves bloomed there despite the heat, mostly blue, and there was an expanse of blackberry by the old fence into which you beat tracks with sticks when the fruit was ripe. Behind the tip as a sort of disguise and well away from the river was a block of radiata pine. Not much grows under pines. About its only use was for raising money. There was always an eager market for the cones, but it wasn't easy work. The sacks had to be dragged out on sledges, or dobbins, to the road.

'Peter's old man cleared out in the weekend.'

'Jesus.'

'How do you know?'

'My dad said after he found out there was something wrong with his throat, he took out all his money and flew to Scotland to find his grandparents' graves without saying anything to his family.'

'Is that a fact.'

'He's flipped then. Tough on Pete.'

'You can say that again.'

'He was always whistling. Whenever I was round there he was whistling. Probably he did something awful to his throat through all the whistling.'

The summer twilights of the bank section would last well after nine and the setting sun glimmer through the western pines almost forever, until at last the navy blue shadows would blur the outlines and separate colours to humped masses of an indiscriminate landscape through which you would jog home late again and leave the morepork calling.

THINKING OF BAGHEERA

'**Y**ou don't much care for pets I know,' says my neighbour. She smiles bleakly across the patio, and sips my Xmas sherry. She is pleased to be able to categorize me so utterly. It won't do to try to tell her of Bagheera, though what she says brings him back to me.

The cat was not even mine, but had been bought for my younger sisters. They soon excluded him from their affection, however. My sisters preferred those possessions which could be dominated. Compliant dolls who would accept the twisting of their arms and legs, and easily cleaned bright, plastic toys. The cat went away a lot, and had for them a disconcerting smell of life and muscle.

My father named the cat Bagheera. My father had a predilection for literary allusion, to use his own phrase. Not that I heard him use it about himself. He was referring to Mr McIntyre his deputy. I remember my father talking about Mr McIntyre to Mum; pausing to preface his remarks with a disparaging smile, and saying that Mr McIntyre had a predilection for literary allusion. I caught the tone, although I couldn't understand the words. There was blossom on the ground that evening, for as he said it I looked out to the fruit trees, and saw the blossom blowing on the ground. Pink, apricot blossom, some lying amid the gravel of the drive, a fading tint towards the garage.

In the evening Bagheera and I would go for a walk. We agreed on equality in our friendship; we would maintain a general direction, but take our individual digressions. In the jungle of the potato rows, or sweet-corn, I would hide, waiting for him to find me, and rub his round head against my face.

The cat brought trophies to the broad window-sill of my bedroom. Thrush wings, fledglings, mice and once a pukeko chick. My father hated the mess. He always drove the cat from the window when he saw it there. Yet often at night, waking briefly, I would look to the window and Bagheera would be there, a darker shape against the sky, his eyes at full stretch in the dusk. I was the only one in the family who could whistle him. It was a loyalty I would sometimes abuse just to impress my friends. Within a minute or two he would appear; springing suddenly from the roof of the sheds, or gliding from beneath the red currant bushes at the bottom of the garden. Beauty is not as common in this world as the claims that are made for it. But Bagheera's black hide flowed like deep water, and his indolent grace masked speed and strength. At times I would put my face right up to him to destroy perspective, and imagine him a full-size panther; see the broad expanse of his velvet nose, and his awesome colgate smile.

In December Bagheera got sick. For three days he didn't come despite my whistling. We were having an end-of-term pageant at school and I was a wise man from the east, so I didn't have much time to look for him. But the day after we broke up, I heard Bagheera under the house. I talked to him for more than an hour and he crawled bit by bit towards me, yet not close enough to touch. I hated to see him. He had scabs along his chin; his breathing made a sound like the sucking of a straw at the bottom of a fizz bottle. He wouldn't eat anything and just lapped weakly at the water I brought, before he backed laboriously again into the darkness under the house.

Each time I looked, his eyes would be blazing there, more fiery as his sickness grew, as if they consumed his substance.

My father decided to take Bagheera to the vet. He brought out Grandad's walking stick and said that he'd hook the cat out when I called him within reach. How easily the cat would normally have avoided such a plan. My father pinned Bagheera down, and tried to drag him closer. Bagheera rolled and gasped before he managed to free himself and creep back amongst the low piles. He knocked an empty tin as he went. It was the tin from the pears I had stolen after being strapped by my father for fishing in my best clothes. When the walking stick failed, my father lost interest in the cat. He had given him his chance and after that he put the matter out of his mind. My father possessed a very disciplined mind. I couldn't forget though, for Bagheera had become my cat. At night I would look to the window, but his calm presence was never there and instead I kept thinking of his eyes in the perpetual darkness beneath the house. Beseeching eyes that waited for me to fulfil the obligation of our friendship.

I asked my father to shoot Bagheera. To put him out of his misery, I said. It was a common enough expression, but my father had no conception of misery in others. I imagine he saw it, in regard to people at least, as the result of incompetence, or the lack of drive. But I kept on at him. I said that Bagheera might spread infection to my sisters, or die under the house and cause a smell in the guest rooms. These considerations, which required no empathy, seemed to impress my father. He refused to fire under the house though, he said. I'd have to coax Bagheera out where he could get a safe shot. He wasn't suppose to shoot at all within the borough limits he said. At the time I didn't fully realize the irony of needing my father to kill Bagheera. I was the only possible go-between.

My father came out late in the afternoon, and stood with the rifle in the shade of the grape vine trellis, waiting for me to call Bagheera out. I felt the hot sun, unaccustomed on the back of my knees as I lay down. It was about the time that Bagheera and I would often take our walk, and I called him with all the urgency and need that I could gather. Even the pet names I used, even those, with the sensitivity of boyhood and my father standing there; for I would spare nothing in my friendship. Bagheera came gradually, his black fur dingy with the dust of the foundations, and the corruption within himself. I could hear his breathing, the straw sucking and spluttering; I could see his blazing eyes level with my own. To get him to quit the piles, and move into the light, was the hardest thing. I was aware of my father's impatience and adult discomfort with the situation.

'Move away from it,' he said, when Bagheera was at the verandah steps and trembling by the saucer of water. My father raised the .22, with which he never missed. No Poona colonel could have shown a greater sureness of aim. My sisters grouped at the study window to watch, their interest in the cat temporarily renewed by the oddity of his death.

The shot was not loud; a compressed, hissing sound. Bagheera arched into the air, grace and panther for a last time and sped away across the lawn into the garden. Just for one moment he raced ahead of death; just for one moment left death behind, with a defiance which stopped my breathing with its triumph. 'I wouldn't think anyone heard the shot at all,' said my father with satisfaction. The saucer lay undisturbed, and beside it one gout of purple blood. Don't tell me it wasn't purple, for I see it still; opalescent blood beside the freshly-torn white wood the bullet dug in the veranda boards.

I didn't go to find the body amongst the currant bushes. Instead I went and lay hidden in the old compost heap, with the large, rasping pumpkin leaves to shade me, and the slaters questing back and forth, wondering why they'd been disturbed. My father and mother walked down by the hedge and I heard my father talking of Bagheera and me. 'I find it hard to understand,' he said. 'He seemed determined to have it shot. Sat there for ages cajoling it out to be shot. And after the attachment he seemed to have for it too. He's a funny lad, Mary. Why couldn't he leave the wretched thing alone?' My father's voice had a tone of mixed indignation and revulsion, as if someone had been sick on the car seat, or one of his employees had broken down and cried. But I remembered Bagheera's release across the lawn, and thought it all worthwhile. He'd done his dash all right.

I lay in the evening warmth, and watched a pumpkin flower only inches from my face. The image of the pumpkin flower was distorted in the flicking light and shade beneath the leaves. The gaping, yellow mouth and slender stamen nodded and rolled like a processional Chinese dragon; the ones they have at weddings and funerals.